# Death of a Ghost

Other titles by Charles Butler

CALYPSO DREAMING

THE FETCH OF MARDY WATT

# CHARLES BUTLER

Death of a Ghost

Illustrated by David Wyatt

HarperCollins *Children's Books*

For Hallie Óg

First published in Great Britain by HarperCollins *Children's Books* 2006
HarperCollins *Children's Books* is a division of HarperCollins *Publishers* Ltd
77-85 Fulham Palace Road, Hammersmith, London, W6 8JB

www.harpercollinschildrensbooks.co.uk

1 3 5 7 9 8 6 4 2

Copyright © Charles Butler 2006

ISBN 0 00 712858 4

Charles Butler asserts the moral right to be
identified as the author of the work.

Printed and bound in Great Britain by
Clays Ltd, St Ives plc

Now like Friar Bacon's Brazen Head I've spoken
"Time is," "Time was," "Time's past."

Byron, Don Juan

# ONE

IT WAS A hot day in August and Jack Purdey was taking the lanes too fast. Jack always drove like that, but today it was worse because the lanes were narrower and he was nervous about Lychfont. Untrimmed hedges flicked the wing mirror and strips of yellow hit the windscreen as a tractor flung back straw. Watching from the passenger seat, Ossian saw his father's profile turn hooked and mean, like a bird of prey in mid-swoop.

Will I have ear hairs when I'm fifty? Ossian wondered. He said nothing, but at each corner braced his foot against the floor.

Jack saw this at last and pointed out in his hurt voice: "We'll be late if I don't put a spurt on."

"We'll probably be late if you do, Dad. Kaput. Worm-food."

"Huh. Morbid child. We want to make a good impression, you know."

A milk tanker pulled out from a gate at this moment and forced them to the edge of a ditch. Jack swore inventively, but he drove with greater caution after that.

All this for Catherine Frazer! thought Ossian. She won't even notice.

Ossian tried to distract himself by reading the book his girlfriend Lizzy had given him. It was a hardback novel with 300 pages of close-set print: *Death of a Mayfly*. Lizzy had slipped it into his hand at Philadelphia International, just before the departure lounge. "For the trip. It's the latest Inspector Gordius."

Nice thought, reflected Ossian. He'd felt bad because he'd bought her nothing in return. Not that she'd seemed to mind.

"Just don't forget me, will you?" she had told him.

The small print made him queasy though, and the plot – some double-cross, triple-bluff mystery about a spy on the run – was too complicated to read in the car. But the message she had stuck in the flyleaf was sweet. "To my Ill-made Knight. From Your Belle Dame Sans Merci." Typical Lizzy, quoting poetry at him. He could see her nose wrinkling as she wrote that.

*"There's a speed limit in this country!"*

"Sorry," said Jack. "For a moment I forgot which side of the road I was meant to be on."

Ossian checked his seat belt for the hundredth time and thought again of Lizzy, back in Philadelphia.

Maybe that quote was just a way of trying to confuse him. Lizzy loved the idea of being beyond his comprehension, a wild and mysterious muse, even if she did have freckles. "You'll never understand me," she would say wistfully. She had talked like that a lot in the week up to his leaving. "And I'll miss you so much, Ossian. Why do you have to follow your dad back to Britain anyway? Just because his residency's ended. Anyone would think he owned you."

"Got no choice, Lizzy. I'm only sixteen, remember. A child in the eyes of the law."

"Not from where I'm standing," smirked Lizzy and wrapped her arms around him.

Stretched out in his car seat, Ossian remembered just how good that had felt. He let Lizzy's hands run down his body once again – then caught an accidental glimpse of his face in the sun-visor mirror. A young man's face, he assured himself. Not a child's at all.

More than once he had suggested Lizzy should come to England too. Or come in a year once her course was over and he was settled, and they would move in together and he'd get a job somehow.

"You really think I'd leave this? It's my home!" she had said, gesturing to a landscape of river, tower and sky.

"You could come back to visit," he said, "whenever you wanted."

"That wouldn't be the same. Like I said—"

"I'll never understand you!"

"Something like that, errant boy," said Lizzy with a sigh.

Ossian wanted to find her sigh mysterious, if only to oblige her, but those freckles stood in his way. In any case, Lizzy was better than mysterious: she was truthful and kind, and she didn't think of him as a famous artist's son first. And she was fit! Yes, he would miss her badly.

The sun was high now and he pushed the sun visor back. There, ahead of him on a ridge of low hill, was the Corn Stone. Ossian had contrived to forget all about it, but it started a domino trail of memories – Lychfont memories, of which this stone was the first. The Corn Stone had been a sacred place once. Many years ago – seven, was it? – he and Colin Frazer had made small but bloody sacrifices there. Little yobs! No vole or shrew had been safe. But now the Stone looked disappointingly mellow, a little pearl button sewn on to the corduroy fields. To Ossian's eye, grown accustomed to life on an American scale, it was as flat as a tiddlywink.

Travel broadens the mind, he reflected, the way a rolling pin broadens pastry. It had certainly flattened

Hampshire. What could Lychfont offer when you'd seen Niagara and the Grand Canyon? Some pleasant ripples of green hill – a ruin or two? A distant prospect of Southampton docks? Perhaps he could have found a way to stay with Lizzy if he'd wanted to. If he'd really tried.

"We should be there by now," said Jack. "I wonder if I've overshot the road? Easily done."

"No, Dad – we'll get to Marlow's Farm in a moment. Then it's less than a mile."

Sure enough, the next bend revealed Marlow's Farm, the tyres on the silage clamp and a field of Friesian cattle.

Ossian had only been to Lychfont once before – that summer with Colin – but he found he remembered every gate and hedge, every dip in the road. Expected them, in fact. They slotted neatly into his mind like puzzle pieces. It was a strange sensation and he searched for the phrase to describe it. Not *déjà vu*, though that came close. More like—

"Bloody cats!" cursed Jack, narrowly avoiding a ginger one as it dragged a twitching pigeon to the ditch. "You'd think they owned the place!"

It had been the summer after his mum left, the summer of Jack's first Royal Academy exhibition, the summer Ossian had turned nine. Catherine Frazer, already making a name as a patron of the arts, had taken pity on the abandoned painter and his son and given them the run of Lychfont for two months. It had been kind of her – although had she and Jack been having an affair, Ossian wondered? It hadn't crossed his mind at the time. If so, it must have ended badly; they hadn't been asked to Lychfont since. Until this new commission.

"Cathy likes her artists up and coming," said Jack when the email reached him in Philadelphia. "I'm surprised I still qualify."

No wonder he was nervous.

Falling with the road into a sudden trench of shadow, Ossian saw the Corn Stone disappear below the horizon for a moment. When it rose again it was no nearer, but tangled behind a nearby church wall. Just a wall, no church. A stairway was hacked into air. There was a solitary arch. Grass curled against the pillars where they lay. That was Lychfont Abbey, a gaunt Reformation ruin. And in the distance, still topping its ridge next to a line of birch, sat the Corn Stone.

Except that now it did not look so pearly or so low. Now it looked like a grey box, blue-grey, almost metallic. And the top of it was smooth. All the better for laying out corpses, Ossian reflected. He should know.

A series of black-and-white chevrons pointed to a sharp curve ahead. *Concealed Entrance.* Out of the sun the road seemed smoky-dark and Jack reached up to adjust the visor. Again, Ossian tried to interest himself in Lizzy's book. Then something made him look up.

"Dad! Look out!"

A large animal – too big for a dog – had run in front of them. A pony had wandered on to the road. It had a pony's shaggy head and fetlocks.

But ponies do not stand so four-square with flame-red eyes and a mouth all dripping crimson.

Jack, with one hand on the wheel and two lunchtime ciders in his belly, saw it just too late.

*"Jesus!"*

The car flipped off the road, clearing the ditch with a powerful thud on the back axle. Jack and Ossian both lurched forward with the shock. Ossian's seat belt did not prevent his forehead hitting the windscreen, though the fabric bit savagely into his neck. Immediately, a dampness began to spread down his face and Lizzy's book was sprayed with red. Jack was stamping at the brake pedal, swearing. Yet the car was still moving, fast enough to take out the wooden gate up ahead. Beyond it, on the yellow grassy mount in the middle of the field, the Corn Stone glinted. The wheels jolted from rut to rut of the baked earth – and when Ossian looked again the Stone was nearer and larger. There was someone lying on it! And they were almost – it was—

"Look out! Dad! We're going to—!"

"I can't! I can't!—"

SULIS AWOKE THAT morning with the sudden knowledge that she was alone. A fire curled in the grate. The sun, flicked by the stiff-fingered trees outside her window, scattered light across her face, lap and feet. But the bed was cold.

"Husband!" she cried out. She sat up, tense and frightened. Angles of sharp sunlight slid over her skin as the white sheets fell from her. "Husband! Brother!"

There was no answer. Ossian – her brother, her husband-to-be – was no longer there. Only the forbidding busts of the immortals by the hearth. She rang for Alaris.

Alaris wafted into the room. A shimmer of rose and sandalwood announced her. "Yes, mistress?"

"Where is Ossian?" Sulis demanded. Her voice was steady, but the intensity of it made Alaris tremble. "Did he go hunting again?"

"N-no, mistress. I haven't seen him since yesterday when he was resting in your ch-chamber."

"Don't lie to me, Alaris! I have to know. Did Ossian leave the house this morning?"

"I h-have not seen him, mistress. I've been in the kitchen since an hour before dawn and have seen nothing."

"Then call the head groom! And the chief huntsman! I must know where he is! Saddle my grey mare!"

"At once, mistress!"

Sulis panted with the effort of being so afraid. Her heart pounded and, as Alaris left, she fell back on her pillow of swan's-down. Ossian gone! And today of all days! Someone must surely have abducted him. But the blank walls denied it and the fireplace opposite leered back at her with blackened teeth.

The head groom and the huntsman came. She heard the grey mare stamping on the flags in the court below, bells jangling on its bridle. No one knew where her husband (as good as) might be. On this, their wedding day! Bridal bells! She threw vases at groom and huntsman, and watched them shatter on the wall above their cringing bodies. Ordinarily, she would have derived some satisfaction from this, but not today.

"You're all *useless!*" she screamed, and leapt across the marble floor to the curtain of her antechamber.

Sulis stormed from room to room. Servants cowered in doorways as she passed and they muttered low what everyone but Sulis already knew. That Ossian had stolen away by night – stolen *himself*, for he was Sulis's property in every way that mattered – and made for the mortal shore. Later, they found her in one of the garden walks, looking through a trellis of vines towards the milky river, weeping.

"He would never have left me," she said. "Not Ossian; we were made for each other. He knows that."

By the middle of the morning she had gathered herself and a painstaking search of the house was under way. Chimneys were being peered up. Long-sealed cupboards were having their locks levered off. The kennelmaster was sniffing with his dogs around the riverbank and the mudflats were being scoured for Ossian's prints. Sulis immured herself in her osier tower, scanning the horizon for signs of movement. The tower was built upon a willow island and a willow ladder led to it from the ground. In this floating bower, Sulis sat until Alaris came, out of breath from the climb, some two hours later.

"There is no sign of Ossian, my lady."

Sulis grunted. "Then despair must be my portion!"

Alaris was tactful enough to wait a good ten seconds before adding: "But I have heard that a seeing-man – a scryer – is lodging near Lychfont."

"A mountebank!" Sulis muttered. "What of it?"

"He has a good reputation, mistress. They say he can set a bridge between the worlds as easily as I can wring a shirt. He has not only knowledge but power too, and... oh, elegant devices! If he is all they claim he might even be able to help you find Ossian." She hesitated shyly before daring to ask: "Shall I send for him?"

"And hold up my shame to public scorn?" said Sulis, as if hearing her for the first time. "Certainly not!"

Sulis had no use for scryers. Most of them were frauds, and even when their talent was genuine they were infuriating, either secretive to a fault or else so garrulous (in a riddling, unhelpful sort of way) that one soon longed for silence. Nor was the whiff they brought with them of other worlds, to her mind, a charming feature. "No," she repeated thoughtfully. "We must find Ossian ourselves. Make a further search of the cellars."

A little later, though, Sulis's bell summoned Alaris back to the willow tower. She entered nervously, and breathless again, having run from the far side of the estate. The goddess was staring into her palms as though they were flawed crystal.

"Y-yes, mistress?"

"You still haven't found him," said Sulis. It was not a question.

"No, mistress."

"I know what you think. You think he has taken off, abandoned me."

"I do not think," said Alaris abjectly. "I obey. But may he not be lost? He may have lost himself and be searching for you even now!"

"He may," agreed Sulis with brief interest. But her turquoise eyes were hooded and cast down. "It makes no difference. Without my aid he will never find his way back." She sighed a lonely sigh. "Do your worst then, Alaris. Summon this scryer of yours. We'll see what he can do."

"At once, mistress."

"But remember..."

"...Yes, mistress?"

"I submit to this only because my honour compels me. If the scryer fails to please me, I will remember who brought him to my house."

"Of course, mistress," said Alaris, and made herself busy straightening the hanging fronds in the doorway. But her fingers were trembling.

"You understand, Alaris," said Sulis grimly. "Excellent. I thought you would."

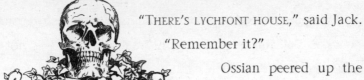

"THERE'S LYCHFONT HOUSE," said Jack. "Remember it?"

Ossian peered up the drive, where half a dozen Jacobean chimneys were showing just clear of the trees.

"Never thought we'd get here in one piece," he said.

"Humph. Do I detect some slight criticism of my driving technique? Be honest."

Ossian looked at his father steadily, remembering that heart-stopping skid back near the Corn Stone. "How long have you got?"

Lychfont House was large, but Ossian did not feel as if he were entering a stately home, despite the marble stallions rearing at the gates. It was simply an old house with more bedrooms than people, and a driveway long enough for a change up to second gear. Catherine Frazer was just lucky to have inherited something she could never have earned honestly. Luck didn't make her stately.

Ossian might not have bothered with these thoughts had it not been for his father's edginess. Something about Catherine had the power to make Jack nervous. Was it only the dangling prospect of future commissions that unsettled him?

Here came Catherine now, glancing across the forecourt in a sky-blue sun dress, a hat of Van Gogh straw.

"So you made it!" she exclaimed, as though that were a wonder. "How marvellous. Are these for me?"

Jack presented her with the bunch of inadequate carnations he had bought at the service station. Ossian prepared to wince, but Catherine – such good manners! – managed to look as if he had handed her the Golden Fleece. "I'll put these in water right away. Ossian! You've grown up, of course. I wouldn't have known you!"

Ossian got through the introductions. Catherine offered her cheek, taking him lightly by the wrist. The smell of peaches and apples engulfed him for a moment, and with it something else that he had forgotten about Catherine, though now he saw it had always been there, and he rather thought it was whisky.

Colin Frazer was standing at the door. Colin had grown too and his hair (which Ossian remembered as golden and curly) was cut short. He loped down the drive to meet them, with a lazy, bouncing stride. Jack was listening hard to Catherine's advice about the roadworks on the way down and how he could have avoided them. "But you're here now," she concluded, "and I can't imagine better weather for it. Where's Sue got to, Colin? She ought to be here."

"She'll appear when she feels like it, I expect. Why are you all standing out here like garden gnomes? It's cooler inside, and there are jugs of juice and Pimms. Coming, Ossian?"

Ossian followed. The sun was bright and Colin became all but invisible as he passed into the porch. Ossian did not remember the heraldic lions on either side of the door, nor their mossy yellow tongues, though they must have been standing guard for decades. But the odd smell of must and polish in the hall itself was instantly recognisable. There was the long gilt mirror and Stubbs bay, and the hanging tiger rug that had always looked at him with such fierce resentment.

Colin led him into the saloon. This was just as Ossian remembered it: the mah-jongg set, the Cluny cushions sewn with unicorns and maidens. Each shelf, sill and tabletop was given over to roses, to irises and orchids, and everywhere hung sprays of fragrant mock orange. Ossian cringed again at the thought of Jack's carnations. Here too were the paintings Catherine's family had gathered on their travels: eighteenth-century mythological oils mostly, with a preference for forests, fountains and plump Arcadians.

"All breasts and blushes," said Colin in a worldly way, following Ossian's gaze to a picture of Venus and Adonis. "Have you ever seen so much blubber?"

"I was just thinking," said Ossian, "about the painting Dad's going to do. You know that's why we're here?"

"God!" Colin clapped his hand to his forehead. "Don't tell me she wants him to produce something like this?"

"Kind of. It's supposed to be a picture of a shepherd tending his flock. Green hills and blue skies, but with jet planes and tractors in the background. Old-fashioned but updated, see? A sort of joke. They're calling it *The Golden Age*."

"I should have guessed," groaned Colin.

"I'm going to be the shepherd, actually. Dad's asked me to model."

Colin shook his head. "I hope he's paying you well."

"Not bad," said Ossian. "He's quite generous like that."

The pay can be very good, he thought. He had been modelling in the life class at the college in Philadelphia when he'd first spotted Lizzy. She'd been wearing a loose shirt knotted at the front and an expression of concentration which made her freckled nose wrinkle. He'd known right away she would be special. She'd caught him frighteningly well.

"I'm only there to make the scenery look good."

"Bloody artists, eh?" said Colin cordially. "You hungry, by the way?"

Ossian followed Colin to the kitchen, wondering where the other guests might be. "I saw several cars in the drive."

"Yes, it's a party," said Colin, helping himself to an olive. "My mother's got some of her horsey friends down – she wants advice on a roan she's had her eye on. There's you and Jack, of course. Oh, and a bunch of money-men Dad had to invite. Something to do with his marina project, I think."

Colin was already on his way out to the lawn. He was carrying too much weight, Ossian noted. His chin barely existed. Was this really the boy he had idolised that summer – the sacrificer-in-chief? At eighteen he seemed virtually middle-aged.

Once, these grounds had boasted peacocks. Ossian remembered being frightened of their strangulated cries, the locust-dry rustling of their fans. Now the lawn was bare, except for the pedestals with their Greek statues that arced to the lake. Things had slipped a bit at Lychfont, he concluded. Zeus and the Olympians were mildewed and rather sombre: Athena in her helmet, Hermes alert as a deer, Pan fluting. Silenus had lost half his grapes in the storms the previous autumn. Yet still they hung on in the alien northern air.

He found Catherine and the other guests listening attentively to Jack.

"It's good to be back," he was telling them. "You can be as cosmopolitan as you like, but you forget how much you'll miss those little things. Marmite, you know, and the shipping forecast."

"Well, you've caught the tan but not the accent – much the best combination. How long were you in the States again?"

"Eighteen months."

"Enough to see the place in all its moods then. To be a traveller rather than a tourist."

A small, sunburnt man in a checked shirt said: "The difference being what?"

"Money, I think. Or time."

"More a question of where you keep your souvenirs – in your hand luggage or in your head," said someone sagely.

"Or on canvas, of course. What do you have to show for your stay there, Jack?"

Jack cast his gaze modestly to the ground. "Most of the originals are still on exhibition back in Philly, but I have some smaller canvases in the car."

"I look forward to seeing those," said Catherine. "Not a day passes but I find something new to admire in the little watercolours you did when you stayed before. I hung them in the saloon, you know. You never painted better, Jack."

Jack acknowledged this with a small, self-mocking bow. Ossian knew he would not care for the suggestion that his best work was seven years behind him. Jack Purdey had once been the *enfant terrible* of English landscape painting, but somehow he had never quite made it to the farther shore and become a Pillar of the Establishment. These days all compliments were routinely sifted for nuggets of treacherous dispraise.

As soon as he could, Ossian escaped back to the house. He felt suddenly and deeply tired. It was the effect of the flight, he supposed; he wasn't used to the time difference. Already he wished he had not come.

And he knew he ought to write to Lizzy.

THE SCRYER'S NEXT question was a delicate one. "May I take it, my lady, that you loved this boy?"

"I do. Even now I do," said Sulis.

"In the way of chaste desire or are there... *other* feelings involved?"

Sulis bridled at the man's insolence. "Does it make a difference?"

"In such cases, invariably," said the scryer with a fatherly smile. "The currents that run between our realm and his can easily be disrupted by such intimate attunements."

"I see," said Sulis coldly. "Well, you may put aside all such worries in this instance. My feelings are vast and profound as any ocean, but they are mine and I control them as I see fit."

The scryer, who had not yet been paid, assured her that everything was quite in order.

"Then we should begin," she said.

They were standing in the flagged kitchen at Lychfont: Sulis, the scryer and the scryer's clerk. The servants' table had been heaved aside and a dusting of chalk laid down, with heaped ridges of ferrous ash trowelled and footed into shapes appropriate to the scryer's trade. Sulis recognised them as letters, but could not read them. They were Syriac, she supposed, or Hebrew.

The scryer felt about in his gourd for the dice and knuckle-bones. The curtains were drawn close and the room was sparkling with the reflected glitter of the ash. At a certain point, Sulis noticed that the scryer had begun to sway slightly back and forth, and that an obscure dribble of language was falling from his lips. Again, the speech was unknown to her. She guessed, though, from certain familiar names studding it, what the scryer was about. It was an invocation, though of what quality she could not yet tell. She suspected the man was a quack.

The scryer's clerk was tapping the gourd, across one end of which the belly skin of a pig was stretched tight. It was quite mesmeric, Sulis had to admit. That, however, was something to beware of. Sometimes these scryers claimed to have fetched out spirits with such rhythms as this, when all they had done was plant a dream in fuzzed and puttied imaginations. It was a trick of the trade.

"Now cast your mind like a net," said the scryer. "Cast through time and space. Don't be afraid."

"I'm not afraid!" cried Sulis.

"Don't be complacent either," he returned without breaking rhythm. Sulis felt as if her response had been expected, required – almost a ritual phrase. Anything she said would sink into the rhythm of that gourd and the old man's chant as completely as a stone tossed on to the Lychfont mudflats. Trick of the trade? There was certainly movement on the ash-strewn floor. It was – *jiggling*, somehow. Then it stood stark and stiff, like filings magnetised but shifted to a new pattern. The ferrous dust no longer spelt out letters. It now formed – what?

"Is it a map?" asked Sulis.

"One moment!" said the scryer's clerk. "Silence now, please. Now my master walks the frayed rope between two worlds."

Better than a circus! thought Sulis mutinously. All the same, she admired the way the scryer still held his rhythm clear of their words. It was dextrous, if a little sinister.

A moment later there was a raucous croak in the rafters overhead. Looking up, Sulis saw a raven.

Charlatan! she thought. An obvious plant!

Perhaps, but the raven was her true totem bird and who but she knew that? Thereafter, it could be heard commenting throatily on the whole consultation.

"Each line shows a way to your man of dust, your Ossian," said the scryer. "From where he has gone there is no easy return, I think. He has been..." The scryer seemed briefly at a loss. "How can I put it in a way that won't seem too alarming?"

"I'm paying you for truth, not tact," said Sulis. "Are you saying you don't know where he is?"

"On the contrary, lady. I know very well. Only he is not all... in one place."

"What do you mean by that? Has he been dismembered?"

"Not exactly. Not physically, that is. But he has been scattered, all the same. Scattered like light through a prism.

It is the effect of the flight, the difference in time. To put it bluntly, the boy you seek is no longer a living person."

"*Oh!*" exclaimed Sulis in alarm.

"Do not misunderstand me. One might say he is alive several times over. There are many Ossians. I see his face reflected back in the stream of time at myriad angles."

Sulis had recovered herself. "Then let us by all means cover every angle," she said with laboured patience.

The scryer looked troubled. "You are aware, no doubt, of the difficulty of a retrieval from history in even the most propitious circumstances. When the subject is in a known location and there are plain tokens of his wish to return, when the signs have all been agreed in advance – even then there is no guarantee of success. I have known cases where what was recovered was mad, or terribly deformed—"

"He'll have to take the risk. He owes me that. Is this all you have to say against the operation?"

The scryer gave another of his embarrassed laughs.

"It's all right," said Sulis impatiently. "I realise it will mean more gold. Just tell your clerk to prepare the equipment."

The raven fluttered down from the rafter and sat on her shoulder. It croaked – encouragingly, Sulis thought.

"I cannot do it yet. No, lady, put away your gold, this has nothing to do with money – though the process is expensive and in due course an adjustment of my fee will no doubt be required. But the technical difficulties are formidable. You wish to find Ossian? Then in each of the places where he now dwells you will need to assume an appropriate form. To determine that takes time."

Sulis sighed. Why did scryers insist on expressing themselves so elliptically?

She was sure that money lay at the root of it. A few more minutes and the scryer would go stiff and start speaking gibberish. Then she would be asked to lay out extra on one of those interpreting women, always so gummy and unhygienic, to render him intelligible. Such a racket!

However, the scryer showed no sign of stiffening just yet. "I can help you to enter Ossian's sphere of existence, once the proper observances have been made. Your way, however, lies by the path of oblivion. In passing through it you must learn to suppress – *partially* suppress – your higher nature."

Sulis was poised to take offence. "What are you saying? That I should put aside my divinity?"

"For the noblest of reasons, I assure you! Ossian is located in a particularly impoverished environment, one that will not sustain a person of your great eminence without peril. I can place you there, of course..."

"But what?" prompted Sulis stonily.

"But not in your – habitual form."

"I don't care what form I assume. I shall manifest myself, claim Ossian and be gone. If the people yield him up without fuss, I may even plant a shrine among them." Sulis pondered the idea. "A spring of healing water, perhaps. I'm fond of springs."

"A very pretty thought, lady. But it may not be so easy. Should you act in ways that are too obviously divine you will weaken the barriers that separate the worlds, with danger to both. On the other hand," the scryer added with a dark emphasis, "there is an equal and opposite danger: that you will be absorbed wholly into their world."

"Me? Absorbed?" retorted Sulis grandly. "Do you know who you are talking to?"

The scryer trembled slightly at her tone, but persisted. "When you are there, you will belong to the Ossian's place and time. You yourself will not know, except in the most shadowy and imperfect manner, who you truly are."

The scryer had been reluctant to broach this subject and with good reason. Perfect memory was as much part of Sulis's divinity as her eternal youth. But Sulis, for once, showed no resentment. She actually smiled and told the scryer condescendingly: "Not know who I am? That might be possible for certain classes of person, I dare say. I don't think I shall forget myself, gentle scryer. Never worry on that account."

The scryer seemed relieved, but was obliged to add: "There remains the problem of temporal dispersal."

Sulis clapped for a dish of sherbet. "Explain that part again," she sighed.

LYCHFONT HOUSE
LYCHFONT
HANTS

Hi Lizzy

I said I'd write as soon as I got here, didn't I, and tell you about the journey. And here I am doing it, just like the dork you've always called me. The flight was fine. Soggy chicken but I kind of liked it. I even survived Dad's driving — just. The only lousy thing was the direction. Away from you. I don't know much about art, but I know this landscape would look better with you in it. I don't know much about love either, but I *think I'm in it with you. With you but without you. Philosophical, huh? On the whole, I'd rather be in Philadelph—*

Ossian put a diagonal line through all that. How come he was suddenly so gushy? He seemed to have got sidetracked into writing exactly the wrong kind of letter. This wasn't Lizzy's thing at all. She liked to know about people and music and clothes; she liked to hear the funny things people said and who laughed. She liked – needed – to picture it all, as if she were watching a movie. But Ossian did not notice things in that way, or did not remember them; in any case, he couldn't shape them into words. And now he had lost the knack of saying easy, natural things. He drew a picture instead, of Catherine and her friends yakking under summer hats and stuffing themselves with smoked-salmon sandwiches. Social satire on the British: Lizzy would laugh at that all right.

But it wasn't what he'd wanted to tell her. He'd wanted to tell her that he was in love. Why was that so difficult to say straight out? It wasn't as if Lizzy wanted him to be witty all the time. That was one of the things that condemned Jack in her eyes. "I only want you for your body, stupid," she used to say.

He never could be sure how much of a joke that was.

He shut the pen and paper in the drawer of the side table. It was too fine a day to spend in his room. The others would think he was sulking. He went down the short corridor to the bathroom and washed his face. He had to pick his way, for the shadows there contained alcoves in which heavy stone busts brooded, Catherine's collection of noble Greeks and Romans. Julius Caesar's nose came close to catching him in the ribs.

Catherine had moved to a hammock seat, twenty metres from the terrace. Six or seven people were gathered there now, and Catherine herself swung under the hammock's flowery awning, its shadow tasselling the lawn. The sharp sun made the scene unreal. As he stood in the doorway, Ossian tried to sort out which of the guests were Catherine's horsey types, and which Mr Frazer's businessmen. Catherine was being inscrutably polite to all.

"Yes, hardly anyone *has* heard of it," she was saying in response to a query from a lugubrious man whose lip was haunted by a wisp of pale moustache. "The Abbey ruins here are not, of course, to be mentioned in the same breath with Rievaulx or Fountains, but in a quiet, backwaterish way Lychfont has its own dignified tale to tell." Sensing a silence, she added: "Henry VIII always struck me as such a lout, don't you agree?"

Everybody did agree; they had no choice. The lugubrious man's wife had always preferred the Stuarts, she said – much more dashing in those wigs.

"Nothing like being beheaded to give a man romantic appeal."

Ossian, who had been approaching in the shade of the wall, heard the laugh that followed this, a laugh like glasses being chinked, and checked his step. The mention of beheading caused him to grip his own neck and his Adam's apple rose and fell. Everyone in that group must be at least twice his age. And in that time, what smoothing of rough edges there must have been; how ready the world had made them for this sipping of drinks on the lawn at Lychfont House, and laughing tinkling laughs and chiming with the tinkling laugh of Catherine.

Fool that he was, he felt afraid – as if he were nine again. Any moment now, Catherine would turn and see him, wave and invite him to be clever too. And he couldn't – wasn't. He turned on his heel with his face flushing hot in the shadow. How stupid! And he knew they had seen him after all, for Catherine was saying: "Jack's boy? Yes, always a quiet one. Hard not to be overshadowed by Jack, of course."

"Not that it's a competition," said another female voice – but by now Ossian had made the corner of the house and seen the grass bump down in cloddy terraces to the flood meadow.

Sod Catherine Frazer, comparing him with Jack like that. That was all she saw when she looked at him, then: an after-image of Jack Purdey, much dimmer than the original. Or a muffled echo mouthing things that had already been said more clearly, more cleverly, *better*. It was humiliating – but oddly enough, it also made him afraid, in a way that had nothing to do with his father. It made him wonder whether he was real at all. In this mood, he became conscious of the bending of the grass beneath his feet, the play of light on the skin of his eye. He was fearful that at any moment he might unravel, be revealed as a random knot of touch and sound, a net of shadows cast from some place far beyond him.

It was at such times, indeed, that he was most likely to meet with ghosts.

The meadow was dark and lush, shadowed in part by the house and by its own river border of willow and silver birch. In wet weather, the river could break its banks and spread a sudden lake there. You could find minnows jungled in the long grass, a drowned canopy of gnats and thistledown. Here too, wading to the knee, Ossian had once walked with Colin to fish with shrimping nets and chased an eel across the lawn as far as the drooped willows.

How long ago was that? Seven years?

It felt like another life.

Ossian lolloped at a diagonal from the house towards a fence where the Lychfont grounds ended in a field of sheep. The flood meadow was dry now, but still soft and peaty underfoot. All this time he knew he was being followed. The black mullioned windows of the hall behind him were unoccupied and his view up the sloping lawn gave no chance of cover. In the shadow near the house, where the long grass was uncut, he saw no footprints but his own. It didn't matter; Ossian knew. A ghost had drifted from the stonework and latched on to him. Its atmosphere of puzzled disappointment had resonated, probably, with his own.

Ossian decided to be friendly. He stopped. The ghost stopped and watched him staring back up the slope. Its long sickly face quivered like a reflection in a pool. Ossian smiled a little, encouragingly – but his smile shot it to ribbons, sliced its joints like cockcrow. It fell in pieces, then laboriously reassembled itself and followed again, dog-like, without rancour. It tracked him along the fence, where the ground grew flat and tussocked. Ossian had no choice but to let it. It did not mean him harm. It shimmered just behind the grass, a green miasma. He guessed what that green colour meant. This ghost had died violently and young.

At the edge of the wood he stopped and looked back again. The ghost was still there, dogging him at thirty metres. The body was just as thin but more distinct now; he could see long fingers and a belt of tools that clinked silently at each step. The legs were bare stalks of flesh. And that sickly face? Ossian blinked into the greenness of the river meadow rising up behind. The face was yellowish – *brass*. It was a metal face! The long, kind, sickly features were gone and Ossian saw jagged mask holes where no light shone, and brass lips rounded as if to speak his name...

"*Ossian!*" it shouted. "*Ossian! Ossian! Ossian! Ossian!*" Ossian turned and ran back to the house.

SULIS'S SHERBERT was finished long since, but the scryer was still explaining about temporal dispersal. The intricacies of human history animated him as few other subjects did, and his curl of white beard wagged puppyishly as he talked. Sulis listened with patience at first, until the scryer unwisely returned to his comparison between time and a beam of light. Entering a spiritually impoverished world, he told her, was like shining a light on to polished crystal. The light would be refracted into many colours and directions. "A marvellous sight, but one signifying disintegration..."

Before long, Sulis was not even pretending to pay attention. Her mind still ran on the humiliation of her abandonment. Every now and then it came back to her and shook her by the throat, in spiteful little sobs. It made all too much sense. Ossian could never have escaped her except by flying to some vulgar place where her own transcendent purity could not easily follow. And he would certainly pay – refracted, dispersed and impoverished as he might be.

"...so you may find he eludes you merely by shifting to another part of the, er, spectrum as it were."

The scryer was waiting for a response. The point of his speech had been clear, at any rate. Following Ossian would be risky, no matter why. And the old man's concern was genuine, Sulis guessed, for all his ludicrous verbosity.

She looked around her. Lychfont's marble reflected in its extreme whiteness the snowy pallor of her own face, and her turquoise eyes were brindled with gold and lapis lazuli. Two colonnades fanned from where she sat, the space between them crossed with walks and pools and fountains. The sky, as always, was kingfisher blue, the earth her own blood red, and rising from its depths a wondrous perfume clothed the air in dark velvet. Sighing, she breathed the smoke of a thousand sacrificial fires.

It was all very beautiful. And should she give this up, even if only with part of herself, even for Ossian? Although she had laughed it off, the scryer's warning had shocked her. Might she really forget her own divinity? What if she should become trapped in the tawdry sphere of existence where Ossian had taken refuge? She could not bear the thought of being tawdry.

"Ossian always was weak-minded," she said. "He needed me, you see, to keep him steady. That's why we were so perfectly matched." She broke down again and a tear snaked down her cheek: "I'll wring his neck!"

"He is unworthy of you, lady," put in the scryer's clerk.

He soon regretted it. Sulis was suddenly towering over him, her golden hair scraping the rafters. "*Unworthy?* Is that how you speak of my consort, little man? Am I a green girl to be soothed with childish comforts? How dare you!"

"My colleague spoke ill-advisedly," hastened the scryer, stepping between them. "He meant no harm, lady. Pardon his folly."

Sulis moved towards the clerk, whose legs were trembling so that they could scarcely bear him. She pointed one finger at him then, slowly, raised it to the roof. The clerk rose too – ten metres into the air, his feet wriggling. He floated out to the nearest pond, then Sulis closed her fist and let him fall. There was a yelp, a splash.

"Consider him pardoned. And now, scryer, let us prepare the cauldron and the irons. There has been too much delay."

"THAT WAS HIS own fault, surely?"

"Not at all. The poor man just blundered into the wrong part of the forest. Hardly a capital offence."

"You can't expect Diana to see it that way. The Olympians are so touchy."

Catherine's house guests were talking about gods. The walls of the saloon were thick with them. Her great-great-uncle had toured Italy at a time when prices were low and brought back a job lot, packed in crates. Ossian found Catherine and the others examining an oil of the hunter Actaeon, stumbling between green bushes on to the bank of a lake. There, by the light of her own immortal face, the goddess Diana bathed naked with her maidens. The deer Actaeon had been chasing could be seen, its hind flank at least, leaping out of the scene stage right, forgotten. The hunter's face was all surprised embarrassment, delight and fear. If he guessed what punishment the goddess would ordain for his intrusion – to be turned into a deer, chased and eaten by his own hounds – that handsome and rather stupid face betrayed nothing of his knowledge.

"The brushwork on his spear is very fine," said Catherine.

Ossian turned away and gave a jump as he saw Sue Frazer sitting on the sofa behind him. The truth was, he had quite forgotten her existence. He blushed to think of it.

Sue was ignoring them all. She was alone on the sofa, trying to concentrate on a book. Between her fingers, Ossian recognised the broken crosier, the mitre in a pool of blood. *Murdering Ministers.* An Inspector Gordius mystery! It might be a good way to open a conversation. That was hard, though. Sue was not exactly taking up the whole sofa, but her leg was crooked under her thigh, with a knee sticking out horizontally to ward off approach. She did not look as if she wanted to talk.

What was there to say about Sue Frazer? The moment Ossian wondered this, a neat packet of knowledge fell open in his mind. Sue was Colin's half-sister: early twenties, bright, sardonic, keen on horses. It was a cause of continual jibing between her and Colin. Horses made Colin sneeze – a shameful allergy for one born to the saddle and he got teased unmercifully for it. It had always been like that. How could Ossian have forgotten?

Sue had been shielding her face with the book. Now, sensing Ossian's presence at her side, she lowered it and looked up at him curiously.

"Ossian? I was wondering what had become of you."

Ossian stared back. He had seen girls as beautiful as this one – but not many. Colin's sister's long hair was pale, with a lustre as if there were some faint light backing it. Her face was an oval and the corners of her eyes tapered orientally, framing irises that were a greeny sea-blue. But it was her skin that made him gape. Her skin was so perfect as to be almost repellent. She might have been wearing a porcelain mask. Only her eyes were mobile and alive – and they darted back and forth as if looking for somewhere to hide. Ossian felt something irresistibly needy in that glance, something lost and far from home. He wanted to rush and assure her that in him, at least, she had one true friend in the world.

"Any murders yet?" he asked lightly, indicating the book.

"Three and counting," Sue smiled, marking her page with a dog-ear. "Though the first looks like it may be accidental. You've read it?"

"A long time ago."

"Oh good!" she smiled, and made room for him on the sofa. "Now, tell me who to suspect."

Ossian shook his head. "All a blur. It was ages back, like I said."

"At least promise me it isn't Sergeant Rosie O'Shea," Sue pouted. "I've taken a real liking to her. How does she put up with that pig of a boss?"

"O'Shea?" Ossian rummaged for the name. "Oh yes, the Irish sergeant. No, she came back in *Legal Tender*, so you're probably safe."

"Not another Inspector Gordius fan!" said Colin, joining them.

"My brother has no interest in fiction," explained Sue.

Colin acknowledged this with a shrug. "Who needs the extra confusion? Real life's weird enough already."

"But that's just where you're missing out," objected Sue. "With books you can force the universe to make sense. Inspector Gordius always gets his man."

"Well, I'm jealous. For me there's no escape from reality. Is it any wonder my hands are shaking?"

Sue looked at her watch. "Never mind, you'll be able to get a drink soon," she smiled.

"Yes, people always ask about *those*," Catherine was saying, as the party turned to a less mythological wall, where in a line above the piano three small frames were overrun with leaf and bush – souvenirs from the Purdeys' previous visit. "Aren't they lovely? Why, thank you. I can never decide which I admire more – the technical virtuosity or Jack's inspired mangling of his commission. He was asked to paint three views of the house and wilfully chose to misunderstand, the impossible man."

"I can't make out the house at all," said one of the guests, peering into the watercolour foliage. "In fact, this one's very much what I see from my room—"

"That's the joke, though! These are views that the *house* has, not views that *we* have of the house. You see that floating dab of white down there? That's me, apparently. Looking no more significant than a petal."

"Ephemerality then," observed the guest, "is the theme of this sequence?"

"Or, in a different way, endurance," Catherine agreed. "How much these four walls must have witnessed! Yet here they still are, basking comfortably while we scurry around on our little errands. That's what Jack was trying to say, wasn't it, Jack?"

"Oh, I'm the last person to ask," said Jack, rather pompously. "Once the paint dries I disown it. I set it adrift to sink or swim."

"Oh, it swims, it swims!"

"Certainly it does," said Mr Frazer, on a rare visit from his study. Even in his own house he wore a suit and tie, and his bald forehead glowed with summer heat. "Do you know Gluck's work at all?"

Colin took Ossian's elbow and drew him aside to ask conspiratorially: "Fancy dodging out to the King's Head later? You could pass for eighteen, easy."

"He's not luring you to the pub already, is he?" asked Sue, whose hearing was excellent. She rose from the sofa and drifted like a mist to stand behind them.

"Ossian and I are going to relive past times, aren't we, Ossian? We've a lot of catching up to do. Don't suppose you want to come?"

"I'd be too embarrassed, the way you drool over that barmaid."

Colin shot her an unpleasant look. "What did I say, Ossian? A fantasy world."

"Now, children," said Catherine cheerfully, choosing to notice Colin's tone. "They're terribly fond of each other really," she explained to the guests.

"We *enjoy* arguing," agreed Sue vigorously. "It's good for the circulation."

"But it's such a waste of time, darling."

"Time's what we have plenty of," said Sue, taking a pastry from the tray. Ossian didn't see her eat it, but when he looked a little later it was gone and her lips were innocent of crumbs.

Ossian was restless. He moved to the French window and stepped on to the terrace beyond. At once he was ambushed by the heat. He waded through it, hugging the wall where the sun had stencilled a stiletto of shade. A brick arch let him into the kitchen yard, where the house's grandeur lapsed into a random shabbiness, messed with bins and sheds.

In this large house solitude was strangely hard to find and for a while he cherished the abrupt leeward silence. A windowless height of red brick leaned out against the sky to shelter him and shrank the house guests' chatter to a querulous hum. Through the frame of the arch, the flowerbeds and lawns sloped down and out of sight. He took a breath and held it, imagined he could hold the moment too. He felt, for that precarious instant, quite content.

Then the ghosts came for him.

He smelt them, first of all. First came the scent of freshly-dug earth, the rich steam of black earth newly turned. Out in the garden he heard the slice of a bright clean blade, soil angled out by a booted heel. Instinctively, he grasped his neck and at once the earth smell became stronger, colder, a memorial fugue of growth and decay.

"Not again!" he murmured. "Can't you leave me alone?"

Into that empty space they streamed. From jarred doors, unlatched windows they fell in soft drifts and billowed out of the loose soil where the late roses bloomed. Little by little, they became defined against each other, spiralling through the August heat. Now he saw their faces, some of them, bleached and torn faces with the skin hanging open, loose as unbuttoned shirts. One's jaw had been smashed in with a hammer. Another was missing the back of its head; a concave scatter of bone showed where the skull should have been. Two had cords about their throats and between them stood a young man who had been run through with a sword. It had entered the small of his back and been thrust upward, its wraith of blade protruding from his mouth like an iron tongue. None had died quietly.

Ossian shrank from them. They would not harm him, he knew. They were phantoms. But their misery stirred such horror in him that he wished only to sink down and shroud himself in the long grass. They were pressing closer, muffling his face, telling him desperate stories, in whispers thin as water... He gasped for breath and pressed his body up against the wall. When he punched, the faces would swirl to nothing about his fist, then re-form and eddy, settle with infinite patience. Behind him, the door into the kitchen was open a little way. He pushed through neck-high and slipped inside, then turned to heave it shut.

But there was no need, for the ghosts had already lapsed, folded back into the complex shadows of the yard. He looked around the kitchen, shaking, and barely recognised the place. Stacks of unwashed plates towered there and the hanging knives glittered, and by the open window a set of crystal wind chimes sang in brittle whispers. Otherwise, the room was silent; but its silence was merely stifled noise, hysterical. The grandfather clock two rooms away was ticking like a bomb.

"Who's there?" asked Ossian uncertainly, and hoped with all his heart that no one would reply.

No one did. But something began to move from the Welsh dresser at the far end of the kitchen. It was hardly more than a wash of blue-black colour. Halfway down, it reached the meat knives where they hung from their hooks – a little dusty, but still gleaming – and paused. One of the knives swung a little, as it might in a gentle breeze or if some tentative finger were testing its edge. At that moment, Ossian even saw the hand itself, a hand tanned and calloused, but not so very different from his own, blooming out of nothingness and as suddenly tucked back. Then the ghost hurried on, past Ossian and through the side door to the hall. Ossian felt no breeze, but there was a flexing of the air as the room bulged a little to let it pass. He blurted out: "What is your name? What are you afraid of?"

The ghost heard him. It bristled. The light in the hall shimmered behind it, tracing patterns of flux, and the skin on Ossian's arm stood stiff as frosted grass. Then – no, he could not say that he *saw* anyone there, but he heard as clearly as if the voice had been his own:

"My name is Ossian!"

The shadow scuttled from him and was followed along the hall tiles by the clip of nailed dog feet. Ossian launched himself after, almost slipping on the polished floor.

"Careful!"

Sue was just coming in by the same door. She carried a tray of empty glasses, which she lifted skilfully as he steadied himself against the door frame. "Where are you off to in such as hurry?"

"Nowhere!" he said, looking beyond her to the hall. "I'm sorry – I was just – being clumsy."

"I see," Sue smiled, placing the tray with the others on the long counter. Her smile was thoughtful and somehow hungry. "You look like a volunteer for the washing up to me. No, don't duck out. Our housekeeper's gone home for the weekend and now the machine's packed up in sympathy. I'm relying on you."

Ossian still hung back. "I only came in for some water."

"If you turn up in kitchens, you must expect to be press-ganged. It would be nice to have the company, anyway. We can compare Gordian notes – yes?" She filled the sink with an iridescent froth of bubbles and hot water.

Ossian hesitated. Then that enigmatic smile opened and engulfed him. It occurred to him again how very attractive Sue really was. "Of course," he said, as she tossed him a damp Woodland Trust tea towel. "Ossian Purdey, at your service."

OSSIAN FOUND COLIN all ready for the pub. He had taken a jacket from the coat stand and was jangling with coins and keys. His hair was combed back and slightly gelled; he looked nearer thirty-eight than eighteen. "How's your thirst now? Coming to the King's Head?"

"Later," said Ossian. "Maybe."

Colin shrugged amiably and they walked to the gravel drive. He pointed out a gap in the greenery at the far end of the garden. "You know the way? The stile? The path through the woods?"

"I'll find it."

Colin left by way of the lawn and wood, through grass already steeped in evening shade. There a narrow path crossed the unravelled river in five stages, each with a sleeper bridge. Ossian watched him until he had trudged himself down to an ant's height, then turned back to the house.

With the tiger skin behind him he admired himself in the gilt mirror in the hall. He knew he was handsome. He had always had good features, of course, but America had made him rugged and slightly unpredictable-looking in the way girls seemed to like.

Some girls.

"Ill-made" Lizzy had called him. He smiled a little grimly to himself. No one else had ever complained.

Sue, for example, had let her gaze linger on him in the most emphatic way while he'd been hanging cups on hooks. Devouring him with her eyes, she'd been. It was strange, he thought, how Sue and he had clicked. He loitered in the hall a while longer, where she would have to pass him if she came down from her room. But by nine o'clock Sue had still not appeared.

Ossian lost patience. He began to feel restless and out of place, and as irritated as if Sue had stood him up on a date. On impulse, he left the house. He followed Colin over the stile and into the lane that wound through Lychfont village.

There was no one in sight. The houses were set back and forested behind hedges, with just the grey glint of a jeep showing here and there through the leaves. There was a farm shop with a chalk board advertising eggs, fish, cheese and manure. And it was silent – but for a radio voice, distant as rain on a skylight, pattering out music. A jay squawked across his path, but Ossian barely looked up as he walked along the verge, intending – so far as he intended anything – to find Colin in the King's Head. He felt dreamy and vague, and did not care which way he went.

For now, though, he followed the curve of the road, keeping clear of the deepest ruts, and was surprised to find it so thick with dark red mud. Had he missed a turning somewhere? Perhaps he had. But Lychfont was as familiar as— no, *more* familiar than his skin. The King's Head would be beyond the church, with its square tower and its single bell that served for all occasions, and the grove of funerary yews. The inn sign creaked damply in the same low wind, the same snivelling breeze coming off the Solent as ever it had.

His thin legs ached: he seemed to have been walking for ever, through this summer evening quarter-light. Walking towards a vague rendezvous that lay both behind and before him. Senseless thoughts turned in his mind like flocks of evening starlings, and would not let him rest. The lane ran along the wall of the Abbey grounds, with a postern gate cut into the wet chips of seal-black flint. The hatch on the gate was open and Ossian was aware of a small owlish face roosting, cowled in shadow. The Abbot's man. Here they distributed food to lepers and the poor. Soldiers and thieves came too, carrying disease in the precious casket of their bodies. Even malaria was not unknown in Lychfont, bred in the sallow marsh beds of a dank mosquito coast.

He heard the King's army roistering on the shore wind. A ship's bell clanked off the water and Ossian crossed himself. The tide ran swiftly beyond the Abbey, there where the shadows tilt and creep. Ossian hugged his body and ran his finger along the endless Abbey wall. How quick the evening had come on, with just the moon to guide him and the light of the lodge keeper's hatch yards and yards back.

"Go thy ways," he said. "Go, parish pilgrim, beat thy bounds and return."

The inn he had, thus occupied, overshot. That was no matter; it would come again. Meanwhile, he was hurrying on and clutching his thin ribs close. Old Peg was up late making candles and the stench of tallow gathered in the road's dip: a greasy, cloacal fog. Ossian knew, none better, the shades into which any thief might slide like a knife and never be seen. And it was getting late. Late.

THE SCRYER SHOOK his head and backed away from the blackened ash. "No. Too late. It's no good. He's drifted off."

Sulis leapt to her feet, appalled. "How? Can he just disappear like that? Bring him back!"

"Do not distress yourself, lady. Agitation will only delay our work further."

She stalked the edge of the room tigerishly. "Easy words for you! Your happiness doesn't rest in the heart of this... this savage, foolish boy! But believe me, scryer, if I'm denied in this, I'll make your misery my masterpiece."

"He won't have gone far," the scryer continued evenly. "The pull of Lychfont is, I am certain, far beyond his power to resist. If he has flown, it will not be further from us, but deeper in."

Sulis frowned and said after a moment: "Through time, you mean?"

"You have a gift for poetical expression, lady," smiled the scryer. "When you say 'through time' I imagine Ossian flitting about like one of the butterflies in your magnificent palm house. First he is on one branch, then another. Never in more than one place. I, on the other hand, think he is more like the moonlit ocean, shining near and far as the water turns, but *everywhere*."

"I understand *that*, of course, but—"

At that moment, the raven on Sulis's shoulder croaked, then fluttered down and picked its way tenderly through the scryer's ash. Its feet made arrow points.

Sulis watched in alarm – if the spirit map were destroyed, they would never find Ossian again, never! The scryer's clerk flapped his hands and tried to shoo the bird away, his bald head rosy with anger. The raven hopped twice, deposited itself back in the ash an arm's length distant and continued forward, with an air of palpable intent.

"Let it be!" cried the scryer, seeing his clerk about to dash forward again. "Can't you see it's showing us where to look?"

"I knew that bird was a good omen!" cried Sulis. "What's it saying?"

The raven had now wandered out of the scryer's circle and was pecking at a hunk of bread, part of the poor clerk's dinner. Sulis, the scryer and the clerk gathered round, puzzling at the cryptic mess the bird's feet had made of all that ash. At last, the scryer nodded in sudden understanding. He clacked the bag of bones at his waist and searched out a paper on which to scribble his deductions.

Sulis did not hide her impatience. "What do you see there? Tell me, you old fraud!"

"Please," said the clerk. "My master must now be commanding great spirits, monstrous ones, hounds to sniff your boy out through all of time and space."

"So he says," rejoined Sulis sullenly.

"I have seen what they can do," said the clerk. "Their teeth are saw teeth, diamond-tipped, their eyes are liquid fire. And their jaws, once they take hold, must be broken before they will release. They will find your boy, never fear. Are you well, my lady?"

Sulis had turned grey as dust.

"You want him caught, don't you?"

"Of course," said Sulis, but not very convincingly. "I love him."

The clerk knew the breeding of this girl. He was a kindly man and he pitied her. Her love for Ossian he did not doubt. But the union she desired would, in unminced words, be indistinguishable from murder. Ossian would die by the sword, his head still chapleted with flowers, and the blood on the petals would be his own, and the river would take it.

How, wondered the clerk, could love live with that?

On the far side of the room the scryer gave a cry – of triumph mixed with alarm.

"What is it?" Sulis was up at once.

The scryer's lip was quivering in a way she thought ominous. Was this the predicted stiffening fit at last? But at length he mastered himself and his eyes (which had seemed about to roll up into his head) fixed her keenly. "It's as I thought. Your boy has manifested in another time – more than one, in all likelihood. This makes things awkward."

"You've lost him then," concluded Sulis. She had been expecting nothing less.

"Not at all. I know how to find him and how to bring him home too."

"How then? Tell!"

"We must consult an oracle," said the scryer. "It won't be easy. For you, especially, there is some risk."

Sulis fixed him icily. "Is my resolve still in doubt with you?"

"Not in the least. So listen."

The scryer made so bold as to approach her. He muttered in her ear. From where he stood the clerk saw

Sulis's long hair ripple lightly as she nodded. Then the nodding stopped. Sulis was stock still. The scryer's words shrivelled in the frosty air.

"A *head*?" said Sulis at last. "*That* head? Do you take me for some kind of Fury?"

"Madam, if there were any other way—"

"If you need an oracle, use one of mine. I've a very reliable one right here in Lychfont, not at all given to double meanings. I'll send Alaris for a chicken and the brass shears right away."

"It would do you no good, my lady. Believe me, the knowledge you seek is not to be had—"

"No! It's unthinkable!"

The scryer waited tactfully, then resumed his muttered persuasions. Sulis endured it for a little, before waving him abruptly aside.

"No, no, you've said quite enough. You have brought me nothing but misery and heartbreak. I can see it is my fate. Very well then, scryer, you shall work your horrible magic and you shall have your ghastly prophesying head. And don't worry, I'll play my part in procuring it for you. You'll not have cause to complain of *my* cooperation."

"You are generosity itself, lady," said the scryer dutifully, and bowed so low that his beard's tip straggled dustily on the flagstone floor.

# TWO

OSSIAN KNEW HE must be late by now. He seemed to have been walking for ever. The Abbey wall was behind him and the dew was falling, the night dark. He had passed the yew grove and the farrier's, passed Peg of the Willow's, as if in a dream. He had no memory of any of them. And even now he was not home. How his thin legs ached!

Ossian was late, but Adam Price's fire would still be burning. In Adam's house there was perpetual light: hearth light or candle, or else the curious green heat of asphyxiated copper, the sulphurous yellow spirits writhing in blown glass. From the slope of the valley the house was an unearthly sight, a quivering glister through the mist.

Different, of course, once you were within the door.

That was still a half-mile off. Past the Kerney Stone and

the cottages where the King's officers were billeted. Ossian shivered when he heard their hurdy-gurdy laughter and the songs they spun out of drink and dice, their brutal merriment. All that lay between him and Adam's house.

He had lingered too long at the crossroads coming home. It was a haunted place, they said, and Ossian's eyes were sharp that way. But there had been nothing ghostly about the girl singing at the ford nearby. There, where the cleft rock was green with moss and thorn-bearded, she'd been washing a cloth of white linen. A spray of flowers had been spread about the lip of the pool, their torn stems steeped in the water. Again and again she had wrung out that cloth and laid it flat across a smooth stone, rubbing at a stain he could not see. He did not know why he had stopped to watch her. But he had loitered in the shadow as she washed and wrung, until at last she had turned and seen him, and smiled as if she had always known he was there. Stumblingly, he had asked for a drink, only to see her laugh and flick the wet slapping cloth at him. He had woken with the shock of that water, looked up to find the sun low and red-faced as himself, and hurried on his road like one pursued.

So it was dark as he came to the last stretch of woodland. He was breathless here, with the dank, leaf-drowned air, the shivering dew that settled on his skin like fever. The stars blinked and flickered beside a purple gob of moon, but he could see little of the village, just the shingle track winding from it.

He was all but clear of the wood when a tree root caught his foot. He fell heavily and the breath was knocked from him.

The tree root was booted – had a voice – was a man, bending over him. That bearded face was lean as a long winter. Ossian went to put his hand to his chest, but the same heavy boot was grinding heel-first into his palm. A second man stood behind and iron shone from his hand.

"Where has your master sent you, so long after the closing of the gates?"

Ossian's lip jibbered. He could not have answered had he wished to. There was no answer he could give.

"What nest have you flown from, fledgling?"

"He'll not speak," said the second man. "Just take what he carries and leave his confession to the crows." The iron shone in his voice too.

Ossian knew what these were. Chance soldiers, cast his way by an unlucky throw. The King's army was all restless, waiting for the call to France. And now had come the rumour of a conspiracy, with Lord Hungerford's name at the back of it.

The bearded man ripped open Ossian's shirt. About Ossian's neck hung the leopard-punch of his master's brotherhood, the sign of his indenture. The man yanked it sideways, choking Ossian before the frayed leather snapped free.

"No gold," the man told his companion. "Shall I slice his throat?"

The second man began to answer – but his only sound was a liquid yelp of fear. Ossian saw him look back past his own shoulder, eyes wide and white. The bearded man followed his gaze and called on St Alban.

A devil was squatting on the alder bough. Ossian saw its horns and coal-red eyes blinking as it preened itself. It croaked twice, then hopped to a lower branch, gripping the wood with close black talons. The smell of sulphur was overpowering.

The man who had hold of Ossian let him drop and fled back towards the army lights, his companion on his heels. The creature flapped after on leathery wings and, landing by the woodland path, barked raucously at their retreat.

Ossian watched in terror. The devil was crawling now, bat-like and awkward, sliding itself forward on grotesquely elongated fingers until it reached the hollow bole of an elm. It squatted there, dark in the night's shadow, eyes glimmering with dull red heat. It folded its wings in neatly and did not move again. They were alone.

They faced each other until dawn, the devil and the goldsmith's boy. Ossian knew he could not outrun the thing; to brave it would be madness. Exhaustion had made his senses ragged, but he could no more shut his eyes in that presence than he could fly. The cruel teeth it had shown! The weasel shrillness of its call! Throughout the night hours it kept its red eyes fixed on him. Ossian waited for dawn and said all the prayers he knew.

Dawn came, swinging a censer of grey light. Ossian made himself stand. He was stiff with cold and dew. By the elm tree nothing stirred. He approached, to find those coal-red eyes no more than a pair of pimpernel flowers growing from the tree's foot. There was no devil.

But the grass where the thing had planted its feet was a pair of charred black arrows.

Ossian stumbled back out of the wood, down the shingle track and past a field of misty cattle. He did not choose his path, no more than a blown leaf, but in five minutes he was outside Adam Price's door.

Mother Bungay had baked fresh loaves that morning. Ossian's stool had a jug of small ale beside it to drown his thirst. He sat in his place and ate, hungry now he could notice it. Adam too was dressed for out of doors. He must have come in shortly before Ossian himself. Mother Bungay was helping him lever off his boots. His cloak, not yet laid up, was draped across his chair like a thunder cloud.

"You were blessed last night," said Adam Price. He fixed Ossian with eyes that were flint-black, flint-sharp. "That was no devil but an angel of God. And it is God who has protected you."

"I NEVER HEARD anyone snore so loud!"

"Shh! He's waking up!"

"Well, it's nothing personal. Just a function of the angle of the epiglottis to the nasal tract."

"I see. Just how much did you two drink last night?"

"I don't remember much about it."

"Then I have my answer," said Sue.

"My head's fine! Ossian didn't say much in the pub, though." Colin screwed his face up in a parody of concentration. "Now I think of it, he never even turned up."

"You're useless, Colin! Useless!"

"Why don't you ask him yourself?"

"I will when I get a chance. Damn – he's drifting off again."

OSSIAN HAD FETCHED up at Adam's door as a baby swaddled in sooty rags. He had been thin as an icicle. Adam had taken him in, fed and raised him, shown him charity. That was fifteen years since. A good man, Adam, a fair master. Ossian had never seen him drunk nor angry, except in that stern, controlled way when he delivered blows as a sculptor might chip a statue from the living rock, to fashion a man. *Chip, chip* – down came the sculptor's hammer. He had made Ossian lovingly, in his own image. It was his duty as a follower of Christ, he said, to cherish the boy.

Ossian slept in Adam's house, in the loft over his cattle. He was skinny, with a tangle of hair the colour of the straw he lay on. In the last year he had grown tall as well, so that he was forced to sleep with his legs curled up towards his chin, but he liked to hear the grunting of the beasts below and breathe the smell of them. The ass Jerusalem loved him and would eat from no one else's hand.

Adam was a goldsmith. He kept a furnace, and in the red-orange heat he shaped and flattened metal according to his mind. His workshop had thick doors and braces of iron because of the gold he kept inside, but they were hardly necessary. Fear of Adam Price was ward enough. Didn't he have spells to keep the Devil himself at bay? Hammers of many weights and shapes lined the walls, files and rasps and tongs, pincers and scorpers, while under the shutter lay a drawplate with a stiff, four-handled lever for racking gold into wire. The fire and the ram's-hide bellows it was Ossian's job to tend stood at the centre of the longest wall, with the kiln set above.

Ossian's place was at the waxed table. There he would scratch designs of interlaced flowers, ready to drape prettily about the rim of a bowl or goblet. Adam engraved them, spectacles on, his hand steady as a cope stone. Or he would chisel out a martyr's face in cameo, beat gold to nothingness between two parchment sheets, gild wood and plaster, tap roundness into a cup's lip. Mother Bungay, sitting in the corner, burnished the finished vessels with a rabbit foot.

Adam's mystery began with the gold itself. That came from the merchants at Southampton, and there Adam would go to bargain. Damaged cups, rings and brooches arrived, ready to be melted and set in new forms. More often it was bezants and dinars, coins traded from Spain. Ossian would feel the gold press down his fingers, bite the beards of long-dead kings. He mourned the loss of so much good workmanship, even to his own master's forge.

"All things pass," said Adam briefly when Ossian spoke of it. "And the Abbot must have a chalice for his mass."

Ossian knew the stages of that journey. The base metals must be sloughed off, gold parted from silver – a lengthy, careful working with fire and brick and salt. Adam would talk of purgatory then, the dreadful cleansing flame of God.

"All metals long to be gold," he taught, "just as all creatures long for heaven. We burn and scour and strip away their sin, and bring them to salvation."

"As you say, master."

But Adam longed to make gold truly, to teach lead to be iron, iron to be copper, copper gold. Such change was in their nature, he declared.

"If the Switzers' mines were left to brew till Doomsday, they would yield whole alps of gold. The angels would use it to gild the towers of God's city. But we men, lacking time..."

He broke off longingly.

"Yes, master?"

"Lacking time, we must squeeze nature into a narrower compass. Ah, Doctor Bacon knew it."

So Ossian would sit at his table, while his master worked slow-burning experiments from tubes and pots. Occasionally, Ossian was startled by an explosion or a shatter of glass. Adam's fingers would be stained violently, blue or green, but Ossian knew better than to ask the reason. In all his years with Adam, he saw his master's temper vexed only by this – the intractability of stubborn nature, which would not yield her deep secrets to him however he tortured her with heat, confinement and dire, corrosive liquors.

"Who was Doctor Bacon, master?"

"The most learned man since Merlin. Once, when I was young, I stood in a library where all the books were chained and daubed with gold, and I held a copy of his *Opus Majus*. They told me the words had been penned by his own hand. I could feel its power, though I hadn't the Latin then to read it. I trembled, Ossian."

Adam was eloquent on the subject of Doctor Bacon. "He had familiars, devils at his command. He had a head of bronze that would tell the future, and magic to compel it. His art would have raised a wall round the whole island of Britain, if—"

Adam had been animated briefly. Now he saw his apprentice's face – curious, eager, puzzled – and his own face darkened. He drew his hand in front of it as if drawing down a veil.

"Go now, Ossian," he said, not ungently. "I have a work to make."

"How much did you two drink last night?"

"My head's fine. Now I think of it, Ossian never even turned up."

"You're useless, Colin! Useless!"

By now, Ossian was sitting up and staring at them suspiciously. "Have I been talking in my sleep?"

"Not unless you snore in Morse code," said Colin.

"It's time you were up, Ossian! It's gone ten."

Ossian yawned. "Where's the fire?"

Colin laughed. "It's Sue. She's got a confession she wants you to make."

Ossian groaned and subsided under the covers.

"We brought you breakfast on a tray," said Colin. "You can't complain." He put the orange juice and a rack of toast on the bedside table.

Sue, meanwhile, had taken a Sunday magazine to the balcony and was flicking through it, pointedly distancing herself from her brother.

"You would never guess," Colin said, "that coming in here was her idea." He laughed again, nervously. "But Sue doesn't like to get her hands dirty."

Ossian realised he wasn't going to be let off. He crossed to the washbasin and splashed his face. Whatever dream he had been in the middle of when he awoke split and scattered. "So what's the problem?"

"I'll be straight with you," said Colin. "We've come to talk about the ghosts."

Ossian was aware of Sue's eyes on his back. He turned slowly: "Who's been seeing ghosts?"

"Sue has, mostly."

Ossian hid his relief well. "Not you?"

"Me?" cried Colin. "Oh, they wouldn't show themselves to me. I'm much too coarse. Ask anyone."

"He says that because he believes the opposite," Sue added, putting the magazine down fidgetingly, "but it's true."

"Sue, on the other hand, is almost a ghost herself. Ethereal, Mum says."

"From her it's not a compliment," said Sue.

"Don't you think so too, though, Ossian? Don't you expect to find her floating downriver with poppies in her hair?" Colin stepped behind his sister and spread her rippling locks across her shoulders.

"I still know how to punch anyhow!" said Sue, proving it.

"See, Ossian?" wheezed Colin. "Looks like a china doll but fights like a heavyweight contender. She's cold and fair and cruel. The youths of Lychfont are all dying for love of her."

At that Ossian felt – to his surprise – a sudden tightening in his own midriff. "Why are you telling me this?"

"I was hoping you could give us a clue about that," replied Sue. "I've been seeing spirits round Lychfont for weeks now, but since you turned up – well!" She rose from her chair and regarded him unblinkingly. "I know you have the gift. I have it too. You've seen them, haven't you?"

Ossian felt himself blush. Being asked that was like being discovered naked. He hoped, for one moment, that it was just a tease, a guess. But returning Sue's gaze he realised she was entirely serious. Perhaps that was why she had been so alarming from the first. The only other place he had seen eyes like hers – so fired with green and blue, with a faint ring of sour-cream yellow about the iris, a lake of veinless white – was in the mirror.

"Yes," he sighed. "I've seen them."

"In the kitchen yard? Above the flood meadow?"

Each question wrung from Ossian a sullen nod.

"I *knew* it! Oh, Ossian, I'm so glad!" exclaimed Sue with quiet triumph. She looked as if she were about to hug him. Ossian actually took a pace backward, so startling did she suddenly appear. "You don't know how lonely I was, thinking I was the only person round here with any sensitivity at all. Surely you understand! Seeing things no one else can see. Feeling things that make you—" she laughed with dizzy relief "—well, I used to think I must be mad."

"I still haven't ruled that out personally," commented Colin, who had taken Sue's place on the balcony and was pretending to read.

"Shut up, Colin. Didn't you sense it too, Ossian, when we met? A kind of... kinship?"

"I did sense it," Ossian had to admit. Why? Why did he have to tell Sue this, just because she wanted to hear? "I knew right away. But I didn't... *know* that I knew, if you understand that," he added lamely.

"Well, of course I understand! Isn't that how it always is? Isn't it all to do with the state between knowing and not knowing – the thing there's no words for? Don't look so confused! All I mean is, when you see a ghost, it's not like walking into a lamp post, is it? You've got to squint – with your mind. You've got to allow it to be possible."

"I never really—"

"You and me, Ossian, we're different from the others. One foot on land, another in the ocean. I knew the moment I saw you. Soul mates."

Ossian decided abruptly that he'd had enough. "This soul mate wants to get dressed," he said, walking to the open bedroom door. "So can you both get out now?"

"And so forceful too!" said Sue brightly as she left. "Catch you later, Ossian."

After ten minutes Ossian clambered out on to the landing. His brain, he decided, did not take well to pre-breakfast pummelling from Sue and Colin. What a double-act they were! Sue with her sea-green gaze and dreamy voice, threatening and vulnerable by turns. And Colin, amused at Ossian's strangeness and his sister's, hoping to stir the water into stranger patterns yet. Yes, that was Colin – trailing through life like a finger through water, flecking the world with useless bubbles.

Ossian had time to take a shower and find some trousers. The nausea he had woken to was beginning to subside. But he was not surprised to hear a knock on the door. Colin was coming back in.

"Did you forget something?" asked Ossian coldly.

"Forget? I don't think so." Colin hovered in the doorway, as if uncertain what to say. All his cockiness had fled. If Ossian hadn't known better, he would have said he looked frightened. "Ossian, tell me. What really happened last night?"

"I don't know what you're talking about."

"At the King's Head. I was there, you know."

"The King's Head? What makes you think I went to the King's Head?"

Colin smiled quickly. Whatever he had been about to say, he had changed his mind. "Nothing. I must have been mistaken. Happens all the time. Even so, Ossian, I've got something for you."

Ossian frowned. "What's that?"

"Good advice. You'll be saved a lot of trouble if you take it."

Colin came and parked himself on the edge of Ossian's bed. He sat there quite a long time, hands on his knees, as if in a dream. When he spoke again, it was with the air of starting a new subject: "You don't want to take too much notice of Sue, you know."

"Oh?"

"She's bored. All her friends are up in London and she's stuck here waiting for her course to start. She's going to study hydrotherapy, did she tell you?"

"No. And don't even try to explain it."

"When Sue's bored, she can get – a bit fanciful," said Colin regretfully. "Like just now, about the ghosts and stuff. Imagination runs riot."

Ossian looked at him steadily. "You were encouraging her."

"Me?" Colin looked shocked. "Not really – I was cutting her a bit of slack, that's all. Sue isn't the kind of person you can just say 'no' to, not straight out. You've got be a bit subtler than that."

That was probably true, Ossian realised. Sue would waltz past any Stop sign on principle. How *did* you deal with a person like that? Distract her probably. Give her something else to think about.

"All I'm saying is, Sue needs careful handling. She can be very persuasive, and she's got a way of making impossible things sound as ordinary as a loaf of sliced white. You mustn't let – I mean – well, I wouldn't want her to suck you into some fantasy of spooks and shadows. She's good at that."

"Hmm. You seem immune at least," said Ossian dryly.

"I do, do I, Ossian? Well, I'm not!" Colin leapt up, with a sudden, startling vigour. His face looked suddenly thinner, wilder. "And I meant what I said about the Lychfont boys dying for love. Be careful, that's all. Keep those hormones on a leash. It's for your own good." By now he was at the door, but as he left he looked back and added: "I'd say you're just her type."

ADAM PRICE SAT by the fire and cracked his knuckles.

"Our vocation touches that of physician, soldier, judge and priest. What surgeon knows more of anatomy? What judge can so skilfully sift truth? What priest can put a man so quickly in mind of his mortal soul as we can with a nail, a wooden screw, a rope? And when the plans of these great men miscarry, who do they turn to but us? We are the prop that maintains the commonwealth, the stitching that hems their fine garments."

"Yes, master."

In the box beside the fireplace lay Adam's collection of keepsakes. When Ossian was younger Adam would set him on his knee and hold out the glittery things to touch.

"This jewel I had from Master Campion, this from Humphrey of Marlborough," he would say. "Mistress Shore wore this the day they parted her head from her body, poor lady."

The lace was still stiff with her blood.

Ossian liked the jewels and lockets, but he preferred the ivory hilt of a small silver dagger carved with men in drooping sleeves. He preferred the long-nosed ebony monster from Ethiopia and the Cup of Potencies from Spain.

"My gentlemen have all been kind," said Adam. "Few of them gave me so much as a harsh word, even *in extremis.*"

Adam was a goldsmith and an alchemist, but he had yet another craft, another forge. Sometimes a message would reach him from the castle upriver, or the London road would summon him. Then he would put off the leather apron and turn spruce and serviceable. Then his metal became tender, became flesh. It was human beings, not nature, that he put to the question. Adam would not have called himself a torturer – but no sorcerer compelling spirits knew better how to distil truth from that raw matter.

Today the summons had come from the Abbey. Adam took the long leather bag, the one that clanked when he lifted it, and called Ossian from his table. Ossian sprang up; he had never been allowed to watch this work before.

The woman in the Abbey cellar was terrified. Ossian saw her fire-thrown shadow on the far wall and thought flickeringly of the girl at the crossroads. But no – this was just some kitchen drab caught listening at the doorways: probably innocent, Adam told Ossian, having looked her over. Unlucky – idly curious at most. Hers was not the face a conspirator would trust, being too mean about the eyes and broad in the forehead. It was a weak, lascivious combination.

Adam's judgement in such matters was acute, but he was careful in his duty. He began, as was customary, by introducing her to the tools of his craft, the collar and tongs, the talons, the disfiguring harrow.

"Your name is Jane Wood?"

Adam's shadow fell across her, blotting the sooty light from the archway at his back. The stone room stank of piss.

"Y-yes, sir." She could scarcely speak for fear.

"You are to tell me nothing but the truth, Jane. If you lie, I will know. I have spirits at my command that will tell me."

Jane listened in horrified silence. Her eyes darted about. They lighted on Ossian and registered a dim surprise at finding him in such a place, but Adam – a man on whom nothing was lost – explained: "This is my servant. He too will know when you lie. You are not going to lie to me, are you, Jane?"

"No – no, sir. I'll tell you everything."

"That's good. That is excellent, Jane. Together we will find the truth, yes? And – heavens, girl, what's the matter *now*?"

For Jane had given way to fresh sobs. Her body quaked and shivered.

"Don't let him near me, will you, sir? Don't let him come near with those bloody paws and steal me away to hell!"

She was looking directly at Ossian. Ossian had never seen such terror. He slowly realised that Jane Wood, in her imbecile fear, had mistaken *him* for one of Master Adam's spirits. Adam took advantage of the situation. "If you are honest with me, Jane, I can protect you. Tell the truth, and St Michael himself will stand between you and this damned spirit. The truth will be your bright shield. But if you lie..."

He looked solemnly into his beard, into the tangled maze of futurity. There was no need to unknot that riddle. Jane was already clamouring to speak.

"Begin then with the Lord Hungerford. How long have you been in his service?"

"Six years, sir, come Lady Day. My father was an ostler in his stables."

"Good, good," said Adam encouragingly. "When did you first hear of his going into France...?"

Ossian stopped listening after a while. Adam would hurt no one today. Jane Wood couldn't get the words out quick enough. And Adam seemed quite satisfied with the answers she gave – stupidly so, thought Ossian. Had he been paying attention, he would have noted how skilfully Adam managed his victim, directing her by delicate touches, keeping her to the point, and above all restraining her – for in her present terror she would have accused anyone he suggested, and what would have become of the delicate web of truth then? But Adam knew at once when she had gone too far and tactfully drew her back with a gentle word, where a threat would only have made her more extravagant.

Jane knew nothing, in any case. Lord Hungerford had met such and such a one, the French ambassador's man – but that was common knowledge. Alas, sir, she did not know if they had discussed the fortifications at Calais. They had talked of hawking and the recent flood. The Frenchman had drunk an inordinate amount of claret and on more than one occasion she had been obliged to strew new rushes... So her talk ran on. Adam managed to seem interested in every trifling detail.

Ossian wished that Jane had been more obdurate. He hadn't forgiven her for thinking he was a devil, nor Adam for allowing it. He looked down at his hands and assured himself that they were, after all, quite free of blood.

But wasn't there something devilish about wanting to watch others suffer? Something foul and squint?

"Well, Ossian?" Adam asked as they climbed up from the Abbey cellars. "How does this trade strike you now?"

Ossian said nothing, but kicked the top of the step and stumbled in the shock of sunlight.

"Lost your tongue, boy? What do you say to the King's service this morning?"

"You never laid a finger on her!" said Ossian, and was amazed at the note of accusation in his voice.

"Do you *wish* me to put a fellow Christian in pain?" Adam sounded shocked. "The sight of the instruments was enough for her. We should thank heaven for it."

"But you will have nothing to tell the Sheriff about Lord Hungerford," Ossian blustered. "Won't he be angry?"

Adam laughed. "You don't suppose they needed Jane Wood's testimony to catch Lord Hungerford? What you saw was for form. Hungerford is a loose-tongued fool and will trip himself in time. Watch and see."

They returned to Adam's house in Lychfont. Ossian said little that evening. He was busy at his wax table, trimming it with flower-headed creatures whose manes were long, thin petals, whose backs and legs twisted in and out like the fruit trees on the wall of the Abbey garden. He finished the work skilfully, but was not content. Mother Bungay boiled a capon for supper, but he prodded its leg with the flat of his knife.

"You have no appetite," she commented dourly. "You saw more today than you had a stomach to. I told you, Adam, he was too young. I said it would be too much for him."

Adam finished chewing, slowly, before he answered. "Too much and too little," he said. "Little enough from me, in truth. It's what he saw in his own mind that surfeits him."

SULIS PROPPED HERSELF up on a cushion. She felt wonderfully weary.

"A melancholy song," she told Alaris. "A song to sweeten misery. Sing of the river."

"Of course, mistress," Alaris replied.

They had retreated to her morning chamber. Sulis, indolent with grief, stretched out upon the bed. Alaris took her lyre, sat on a marble step and began to pluck out a tune. Her voice was sweet, but Sulis did not trouble with the words. They were bound to be melancholy, for that was what she had commanded. A river, she had said, and now, while her maid's fingers rippled across the lyre, Sulis found her mind drifting, flowing with the river on its journey. Fifty miles inland she rose, a slip of light amidst the chalk and flint. Gargled by rock, she bobbed under the blown grass, hummed fat bees across her banks, ricocheted the dragonflies downstream and followed thirstily to the plain. At length, she became a divider of fields, made way through rich harvests of oats and wheat. Sheep's teeth nipped her shallows and cattle curved their tongues to reap crystal sheaves, while in her silted depths the slick trout threaded pennants of luminous weed. Then, tiring, she slowed and muddled through ill-assorted islets, reserving solid clumps of land for the use of coots and ducks, for the remote ghosts of swans. Sulis shifted comfortably on her pillow. This was Lychfont, her own country. The rushes towered there. No fisher waited, but sieving birds prospected the mud or snatched at elvers. There the flats were loose and salty, lifted and relaid four times a day by the restless Solent tides. And there—

But what was this? Less than a mile distant, misty as giants, stood gantries, cranes and pipes for oil, thicker than a man is tall. This was not her Lychfont. This was urban water, chopped and grey, and it was thronged with greasy traffic. The coast was gashed.

Sulis sat up abruptly and shivered. She scowled at Alaris, who was still playing on the far side of the room. She suspected that she had just had a vision of the place where Ossian – wretched, vile boy! – had taken flight. A tawdry place indeed, with its filth and noise and ugly buildings. She kicked her sandal clean across the room.

Alaris had done ill, there was no doubt. The scryer she had recommended was proving a disaster. He had quite taken over the Lychfont kitchen. Even now, he was occupied with a ludicrous divination involving glass tubes and knuckle-bones, smoke and daubs of bright green paint. In an hour, or perhaps two, he would call on Sulis to help him cast the Oracular Head. Yes – *he* would call on *her*! As if she were no better than his clerk! Only her deep love for Ossian, he had declared, would draw him back to his centre, to Lychfont – to her arms.

Charlatan.

None of that would matter if Ossian could indeed be returned safely, but she had small hope of success. She wondered whether to strike the scryer dead straight away. It might be the kindest thing. Hope had proved a gadfly torment, much worse than dull despair.

Meanwhile, the immortals' busts stared coldly from the far side of the room. The great marble fireplace gaped and the grate was a set of rusty iron teeth. *He is lost*, they seemed to say. *He is lost as the flame that flickered yesterday. You shall never have him.*

What do you know about it? thought Sulis sourly. She glared at all the marble pantheon.

"Alaris!" she cried abruptly. "Why are you playing such a doleful tune? Is this how you think to cheer me?"

"Pardon, mistress!"

"One might think this was Ossian's funeral, not his wedding day."

"I am a fool. Shall I sing a merry song, mistress?"

"Gracious no! Have you no sense of what a grieving heart can stand?" Sulis shook her head. "No, no, of course you have not. Your sensibilities are coarse and common. That is your nature. You are not to blame."

"Thank you, mistress."

"But leave me now. I need to rest in silence."

Alaris shimmered from the room. Sulis let her gaze follow, but Alaris was a blur and Sulis's eyes were rainbow crystal. "Foolish girl," she said fondly, letting slip a tear. "I hope I never have to kill you."

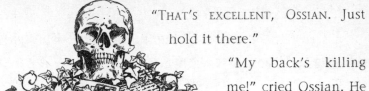

"THAT'S EXCELLENT, OSSIAN. Just hold it there."

"My back's killing me!" cried Ossian. He was modelling for his father's picture, half-naked and holding a makeshift shepherd's crook.

"Don't whinge, we've only been working for forty minutes. Catherine, what do you think?"

Catherine peered critically over the top of the easel. Ossian was stooped in the rockery twenty-five metres away, a pained expression on his face. "Not quite Poussin, is it? And the foliage does seem a very *bright* green."

"I can tone that down later. But look at Ossian – is that what you'd call a graceful posture?"

"The fact he's managing it at all is impressive," said Catherine tactfully. "You look marvellous, Ossian!"

"Yeah... right."

"Listen to him!" said Jack. "Careless ease is what we're after. Imagine. You're a simple shepherd, piping on a rustic flute and so on. Your sheep are behaving themselves in a tidy flock nearby You've bent down to buckle your sandal, when you look back over your shoulder and spot—" Jack turned to Catherine in sudden confusion. "Just what *does* he see back there?"

"A girl, I'd say. Definitely."

"A girl, right. And she's beautiful. Nicest looking girl you ever saw. Get it? Now, bend down and look relaxed but alert."

"How's this?"

"Natural, please! You can do better, Ossian."

"Oh, let him go, Jack. He's too self-conscious."

Jack muttered. "I suppose it wouldn't hurt to give him a break while I moderate the greenery. You hear that, Ossian?"

Ossian stood up a little stiffly. "I'm out of here."

"But remember – you owe me three more hours, at a time of my choosing!"

"Yessir, Mr Jack."

Jack turned to Catherine. "I should probably have him shot."

"Nonsense!" she giggled. "Have him die of love instead. Much more pastoral."

Ossian heard their laughter as he slipped his shirt back on and made for cover. His back was stiff and he stretched as he walked, each limb in turn. Soon he found himself by the topiary hedge at the side of the house. He had noticed it sidelong from his bedroom window, and the ornamental lake beyond it.

The hedge was Mr Frazer's hobby. Each bush was cut into the shape of a bird or animal and together they were dancing a wild conga. Ossian observed them wryly; it was not what he would have expected from Catherine's sombre husband. He squeezed between a dragon and a waddling pig and found himself on a closely-cropped lawn. A shrubbery and an answering cliff of box hedge rose thirty metres away, while to his left the long, oval lake, guarded by a flock of paddling statues, discouraged escape to the house. The fourth way, up towards the wood, the valley's neck was choked with trees. The patch of garden was closed in, silent and stuffy with windless scents. One or two ghosts fled like startled birds at his approach.

He crossed the lawn. Some croquet hoops were set up there, but had been abandoned. His impression was that they had been that way for some time. But a mallet lay waiting, as if it had been intended for him. He thought of the scene in that Inspector Gordius novel where the Rural Dean had been discovered, face down in the orchids with a pruning knife at his side. And how the poor gardener who was first on the scene had picked it up quite naturally and been, for a while, suspected. It had carried his dabs

Ossian lifted the mallet and felt the weight of its head on his palm.

"Colonel Mustard," he said aloud in an actor's voice, "on the lawn, with the lead piping!"

"Too right, Ossian! No room for squeamishness in this game," said Sue, emerging unexpectedly from behind a large, leaf-fleeced sheep. Ossian jumped. Since that early-morning invasion with Colin the day before he had hardly seen Sue, and never alone. She was wearing jeans and a blue silk shirt that rippled in the faint breeze, as though her body were ruffled water. She too was holding a mallet. "Croquet is just chess with hammers."

"You scared me!" said Ossian, who strongly suspected she had meant to. "And I'm crap at chess."

Sue gave a brief laugh. "So we'll play croquet! Get ready, Ossian. Prepare to scrabble in shrubs and prickly bushes."

"I guess," Ossian agreed cautiously, but Sue hadn't waited for agreement. She was already positioning herself by the first hoop. As soon as she gripped the mallet she changed. Crouching, she lined up her shot with the concentration of a sniper; she was obviously an expert. She swung, hit and took the first hoop majestically, like a triumphal arch. Ossian leaned in what he hoped was an elegant way on the handle of his mallet. He knew nothing about croquet, he told her – "Something to do with flamingos, isn't it?" – but that only provoked a shout of savage laughter.

"Off with your head! Just watch and learn."

He had to wait a while for his turn. When it came, he

hit the ball equivocally into the metal of the hoop. It made an unlovely clunk and wobbled.

"Bad luck!" commiserated Sue. After that, she sent him scrabbling into shrubs and bushes according to her promise, but always with the reluctant air of someone who has accidentally run over a small animal and is now obliged, through sheer humanity, to wring its neck.

Despite this rough treatment, Ossian began to enjoy himself. He liked to watch her work, so slim and intent, stooping slightly before cannoning her own ball through the next hoop, or his – with a definitive whack – back into the shrubbery. Ossian came to know that shrubbery rather well. For the fifth time he got down on his knees and burrowed into it, a flail of wild briar combing his scalp. He was aware too of Sue's eyes on his backside. Perhaps that's why she hits me this way so often, he thought. She likes to watch me grovel.

"I'd ask Colin to join us," Sue was saying, "but it's really a game for two, don't you think?"

Ossian found that it was pleasant to agree and see Sue reward him with that astonishing smile and feel her step just a little closer than was necessary to the placing of her shot.

After that, he did not mind about losing – not even when a zealous attempt of his own to hit the peg clipped his ball towards the lake. There it collided with a stone cornucopia and sank.

"Never mind," said Sue. "We have some spares. No," she said, seeing Ossian lie down at the water's edge, "don't be silly, it's deeper than it looks. I'll get the gardener to fish it out. No need to slime your arm with algae. Oh, yuck!"

He threatened her with the dripping, frog-green limb. She shrieked, laughing.

"Monster!"

"No squeamishness, remember!"

She raised her mallet as if to defend herself, and for a moment they were struggling over it. In the end, Ossian wrested it from her, pulling her closer in the process. Momentarily off-balance, he felt the softness of her breast on his palm. The thrill it gave him made him gasp.

"No squeamishness," she smiled, then converted it to a childish pout as she flopped on to the grass beside him. "Oh, Ossian, what were you and Jack thinking of, staying away from Lychfont all this time?"

"Earning a living mostly. Dad goes where the commissions are."

"And what about you?"

"Just part of the Purdey luggage," said Ossian.

"Poor thing!" Sue mocked. "Dragged out to America for a year. What did that do for your education?"

"America *was* educational," said Ossian firmly. "Very."

He smiled to himself. Lizzy had taught him a lot, for a start. He'd been a good student too. "We've never stayed long anywhere. Always going places, Dad and me."

Sue looked at him oddly, the sun catching her green-blue eyes. "And do you ever meet yourself coming back?"

There was something strange in her tone, as if she were giving him some kind of hint. "What do you mean by that?" said Ossian aggressively.

"Nothing!" laughed Sue. "Only that you're very busy. Like you said."

"What? Oh, yeah, Dad's feet are itchy all right."

But Sue was not fooled. "What did you *think* I meant, Ossian?"

He stared at her mulishly, but it seemed he had no choice. "I thought you were talking about that *unreal* feeling, you know?" he blurted. "Everyone gets it sometimes, I expect. Like you're part of another person's dream, maybe, or an echo – still echoing on long after the music's stopped. Not real. You ever felt like that?"

"Can't say I have," said Sue, looking at him curiously. "You poor thing, Ossian. I think you need some cheering up. Come on."

She rose and took his hand, turning back to the house.

"Hey, what about our game?" said Ossian.

"I don't know. I'm not in the mood for that any more."

"What's the rush, Sue?"

"Hunger. You make me hungry and I just saw the time. Come inside and I'll introduce you to my Welsh rarebit."

"It's barely gone twelve."

She gave him her most inviting smile. "Farmhouse cheddar... Worcester sauce... Hot English mustard. And, of course, the secret Frazer ingredient. Can you resist?"

Ossian began to follow automatically, then checked himself. Somewhere in his mind a signal was set at danger. He thought of all those lovesick boys – and then of hammers, blood and bone.

"You go," he said, turning back to the croquet. "I need to practise."

Sue bridled. Ossian saw it as he lined up his next shot with her discarded ball. She was not used to being refused. That gave him a dry satisfaction, though the refusing also pained him – a medicinal pain, like that of a wound being swabbed. Serve her right for making him find her attractive.

"Suit yourself," she said coldly, and wandered to the edge of the wood.

Ossian watched the swing of her mallet as it beheaded dandelions in the rough grass and the way she did not look back. He knew himself to be a small, decapitated flower.

The pleasure he had felt in pushing Sue away fell apart like ash. Why had he done it, he wondered? And what, when she mentioned hunger, had made him remember the ghosts in the kitchen yard?

He became aware of a presence at the edge of his vision. There, amidst the box-hedge revellers, a new ghost was standing, powerful and intent. This was no limp and dreary spirit like that which had drifted after him on his first day at Lychfont. This ghost was flexed like muscle; it almost believed itself alive. And something like branches, like antlers, grew from its head, brown against the green of the hedge. Ossian reeled away slightly, was afraid of it, though he was not the object of its gaze. That was focused laser-tight on Sue and held steady until, sensing it there, she turned and gazed back. Then, with a shiver, the ghost relaxed and patched itself into the sculpted leaves invisibly.

Sue returned to Ossian almost humble, head cast down. And when her eyes met his, the neediness in her gaze made him feel as if he had been presented with a miraculous second chance. Again he felt that bond, that strange half-kinship with her, which made her bad opinion unbearable. It seemed... *fitting* that they should be friends.

"You saw?" she asked quietly.

He nodded. "It was an old one. And angry. Something bad happened to it, a long time ago."

"The way it stared!" She shivered. "It frightened me, Ossian. Please come inside. I don't want to be out here any more." She moved back, away from the hedge. He put his arm around her shoulder. As they came to the edge of the ornamental lake she added in a small, confessional voice: "We've got to talk."

"We've *been* talking!" said Ossian.

"Not social talk! I mean about the Lychfont ghosts." She was edging her way around the end of the lake, where they could only walk in single file. "And what got sacrificed on the Corn Stone, when you and Colin were kids—"

"The Corn Stone?" said Ossian, stumbling after. "Has Colin been talking to you about that? What's he said?"

"You know Colin! He's such a one for dangling secrets. I know he's got some idea in his head about you. But I want to work it out – I've *got* to. Like good old Sergeant Rosie O'Shea, you know?"

She was waiting for him on the terrace now. The neediness was still in her voice, but already Sue looked a good deal less vulnerable. Ossian noticed that he was following her into the house after all. Sue seemed to be the kind of person who always got what she wanted in the end.

"As soon as Mum said you were coming to visit," she explained, "Colin began to hint at something gory in your past. When I ask him for details he clams up, but it's important, I know it is. So tell me the whole truth now, Ossian. Just what did you two do there all those years ago?"

"Nothing," said Ossian, recklessly meeting her gaze at the French windows. That gaze did not falter. He forced the word out again. "Nothing, Sue. There's really nothing to tell."

OSSIAN HANDED SUE a glass of sparkling water.

"It was a game, that's all," he insisted for the last time. "A stupid dare. We killed a mouse and a couple of toads on the Corn Stone, and Colin was High Priest. We were snotty kids, that's all. I don't remember much about it."

"If you say so, Ossian," said Sue, eyeing him doubtfully. "But games can be serious, can't they? They can have consequences."

Even croquet? Ossian wondered. The water had restored Sue's spirits to a remarkable degree. He did not doubt that she was enjoying herself as Sergeant Rosie O'Shea. Sitting beside her on the sofa, he found himself asking the questions proper to a baffled sidekick.

"OK, so me and Colin played at sacrifices years ago. What has this got to do with the ghosts? You look like you've got a theory."

"I think that when you started killing animals on the Corn Stone you weren't acting on a whim. That spot had seen sacrifice before, and not just toads. The question is – *why* were you doing it? Not for fun, I bet. That place had got a taste for blood, way back. It was luring you on." She stared at him, waiting for a response. "Well, Ossian? Does that sound ridiculous?"

If anyone else had said it, Ossian would have laughed. But it gave him a pleasant, shivery feeling, hearing Sue talk that way.

"It's a – strange idea."

"You don't sound convinced. But look at the evidence. The Stone's old. Older than the Abbey. When they were planning the marina, Dad got hold of lots of mouldy maps and they all had it marked. The Corn Stone, Coney Stone, Queen Stone – the name changed. But Dad says it goes back further, beyond any names. And when they started digging out the ground for the boathouses near there, you know what they found, don't you?"

Ossian frowned. "No, I don't."

"You must! It was in all the papers six months ago. But, of course, you were in America. You wouldn't have heard."

"Heard what?"

Sue pulled a face. "The Lychfont Man. Even in a newspaper photo it was pretty unpleasant. You could still see his stubble and the stitching in his shirt. Two thousand years old and he looked like he fell asleep over yesterday's paper. Except for the rope around his neck, of course."

"Someone was murdered?" said Ossian.

"Perhaps," said Sue. "Or sacrificed. Or married to the Spring Goddess – quite an honour really. Not that this chap looked too thrilled. After a couple of millennia with peat up your nostrils, who would?"

Ossian felt himself grow quiet. The ghosts in the kitchen yard – some of them had been strangled. "But how can you have a 2000-year-old corpse?" he began. "It would have turned into a skeleton long since."

"Not necessarily. It's all down to the chemical properties of the soil round here. Skin doesn't rot, nor cloth. Don't look so sceptical, Ossian! It's an established scientific fact. There was another case just like it sixty years ago. Some ditchers turned up a body and at first the police thought he must have died just weeks earlier. They even opened a murder enquiry. Turns out he was a contemporary of Julius Caesar."

"Your Lychfont Man wasn't the only one then?"

Sue shook her head faintly and put down her glass. "Spring's an annual event, isn't it? My guess is these were regular killing fields. Killing *bogs* then. This guy was probably sacrificed for the sake of a good harvest. Now pop to the fridge, will you, and get me a refill." Ossian obliged and Sue smiled her mother's social smile as she took the full glass from him. "All I know is, it wasn't long after that I started seeing ghosts around Lychfont House. And since you've come, the place is positively infested with them, so— What? Why are you looking at me like I was stupid?"

"I don't think you're stupid. Too clever, more like. You're making it too complicated. But carry on. Explain about the ghosts."

"I think you should be doing that, Ossian! You're the one pulling them in like moths to a flame. So what do you say? Any dark secrets you'd like to let me in on?"

"Me? Not very dark, no. Sorry."

"You're too shy," said Sue. "I'm sure you have all kinds of hidden recesses. Like a Chinese box."

"Not really! Apart from being able to – *see* things, there's nothing special about me."

Sue smiled again – but not this time with amusement. She stood, stretched and turned like a window-sill cat as a Hoover moaned overhead. "You're a nice bloke, Ossian, but lose the false modesty. People will end up believing you."

"MASTER PRICE!"

A single horseman was skittering on the dew-wet cobbles. He did not dismount, but whacked the shutter with the knob of his blackthorn. From his roost in the barn Ossian saw the man's starlit face, so thin and meagre, and his cloak wrapped tight; he heard the impatience in his breath as he waited for Adam to appear.

Adam came still dressed, a pair of spectacles upon his nose. His words were curt; he knew this man and did not trust him. They spoke softly at first, then the man sharper – not loud, but the quiet carried a long way in the starry air. "You must come. It's the King's business."

"Must?" Adam stiffened at that. He stepped a pace towards the man's skittish horse. Although the man was mounted, Adam seemed to dwarf him. Ossian was suddenly aware of the muscles in Adam's arms and how they were flexed. As Adam put his hand to the horse, the rider cried out and raised his blackthorn. But Adam was only whispering the horse calm, telling it charmers' secrets. The hooves were still.

Ossian laced his shoes and approached the men.

"But I shall lose my work," Adam was saying. "Three months of tending. Tomorrow would have seen the fruit of it."

The man glanced at Ossian. "Here's your boy. Leave him. He'll guard your fire."

"I'll stay, master. Tell me what to do. You know I'll be careful."

Ossian knew what business the man had in mind. He tried to tell himself it was the cruelty that made him flinch, the thought of red-hot irons searing human flesh – but he was not deceived. The cruelty was all within himself.

Adam narrowed his gaze, as if he saw all the thoughts within him. But finally he turned aside and said. "No. He is my apprentice. I will not travel without him."

"This is not a slight matter," said the man irritably. "The King's safety may be in question. It's no place for a boy."

"He comes or we both stop here," said Adam, unperturbed.

"My orders concerned only you. The Council will be angry."

"Angry?" said Adam. "Yes. If you return alone."

The man bit his lip. He seemed to be weighing things up. He returned Adam's dislike with interest, but Adam was an impossible man to bully. In the end he asked, almost humbly: "Is he mute?"

Adam smiled: "The grave is more voluble."

"So be it. On your head, not mine. What's your name, boy?" the messenger asked, turning quickly to Ossian.

"Ossian, sir."

From Adam's quick gesture of irritation Ossian knew he should not have answered.

The messenger laughed, a soft, midnight laugh. "The dead speak! I've a horse saddled for you, Master Price: take the boy up behind. Can you ready yourself in ten minutes? The journey isn't long."

"I am ready now. The Castle, is it?"

"Then you know something of the business."

"I know Scrope's neck is thin enough to chop."

The air smelt of burning tar from Adam's torch and the sodden, mealy damp of rotting leaves.

"To know more than that would be unwise," said the messenger.

Ossian had often ridden Adam's old packhorse Cib, who had never so much as broken into a trot. The horse he sat on now seemed very high, and Adam had a way of riding that kept him guessing as they picked their way through the stone dawn puddles. They went down through the village, half a mile through the chestnut and elm woods, then to the old watergate of the Castle itself. The gate was disused, its entrance flooded four times a day and levelled with mud – but on this night a causeway of boards had been laid down and Adam, Ossian and their guide trod the silty planks, dismounted and ducked through the half-buried entrance.

"Why did you want me to come?" whispered Ossian to Adam. "I don't trust that man."

"Nor do I! That's why I need you, Ossian, and I'm sorry if danger comes of it. But I understood what he wanted at once. Not a man of skill, just a body to throw to some dogs in ermine and silver spurs. I need a witness to the health of Master Scrope before I begin to question him. So, Ossian, watch everything and do not speak yourself. In this trade every word is a confession."

They walked through a patch of dusky yard, then to a second gate, and up to a floor where the windows were barred with iron. The blackthorn man took Adam aside and left Ossian to kick his heels in a bare, oak-furnished room, yawning dust. Adam returned looking serious, the blackthorn man and two others with him, and they crossed into a larger chamber, Ossian following. In a huge stone fireplace a poker glowed. Five people stood waiting and one sat. There was a table with iron braces and stains in several shades of russet and brown.

"I lack no duty," said a crumple of cloth at the seated man's feet. It moved as it spoke and Ossian saw emerge from it, finger by finger like the legs of a crab, a man's hand. Then the whole heap of cloth rolled over.

The pouch of bloody flesh that hung from it had been a face. Two eyes still sat in its centre, though one was atilt and its skin somehow petalled – a crimson, floating lily.

Ossian could feel Adam tense with anger at the sight. Not pity – never that – but the righteous, professional anger of a craftsman who sees a job botched. Scrope had been half-murdered. Now they expected Adam to finish the job.

"You see why I wanted you here," Adam muttered to Ossian.

Ossian did see, though he dared not answer. Scrope was going to die. But Scrope was Lord Hungerford's man and Hungerford still had friends at court who might seek a person to be revenged on. Adam had been right to worry.

"I know what you are," rasped Scrope through what was left of his mouth. "You're the hangman, aren't you? Here's my neck then—"

"Now then, sir," began Adam in his reassuring voice. "Heaven won't smile on a despairing man, not one that quits his post. Don't be so eager to exchange this life for one you know nothing of."

"My soul is bound for heaven!" said Scrope.

Adam shook his head. "Unshriven, sir, and thrashing in the grip of wrath? I fear the worst."

Scrope groaned. "Just give me a swift despatch and be done."

"Forgive me, sir, I am no executioner. I am a humble surgeon. I wish only to search the black and gangrenous wound of treason that afflicts you."

They talked in this flowery way for some time. At some point they left the state of Scrope's soul and began on the reason for his arrest. It had something to do with Lord Hungerford's part in the negotiations with France. Bribery came into it. But here the talk became tedious, a matter of dates and promises, trips up the Thames by midnight boat, skirmishes and Latin punctuation. At last, it became clear that Scrope would go a certain distance in his confession and no further. He would put his own neck under the axe willingly enough, but not that of his master. Whenever Adam pushed him that way (in his oh-so-reasonable voice, sir, and it would put your mind at ease, sir, to do it) he snarled and called Adam cur, and told him again to slit his throat.

Then Adam sighed as if his heart grieved him, for he knew there was only one way. He took the poker from the fireplace and touched a piece of Scrope's cloak. They heard the sigh of the cloth as it fell away, leaving a hole that glinted with cinder and sour smoke. Adam looked at Scrope for the last time, questioningly, with one brow raised. Scrope, understanding him, gobbed spit and blood – only to hear them fizz to steam, neatly fended on the poker's tip.

Scrope made no sound as the iron went to meet his thigh. His face squelched out a little more blood as the muscles contracted, but he would give them no more satisfaction, not a whimper. The smell of burnt flesh he could not prevent. It reminded Ossian, to his disgust, that he was hungry. He thought of crackling and roast pork. The man with the blackthorn had hidden his nose in a scented handkerchief, in fastidious disgust. But Ossian knew that he was laughing.

Going homeward, Adam did not speak. He had received absolution in St Dunstan's chapel and prayed his fill, but the day's business could not have pleased him. Behind lay Scrope's body, useless as a flooded mine, holding secrets that could never be recovered now short of necromancy. Before lay the ruined work of six months. The fruit of his alchemy was dust. So much for the liquors carefully distilled, heated by minute calibrations to the just degree, the precious ingredients hazarded and lost, the hope and ingenuity, the faith, the cost.

Adam said nothing of any of it.

Ossian did not try to assuage his master's silence. There was nothing he could have said. Any word he tossed on that cheerless fire would have been consumed at once, without heat or light.

But later that day Adam gave him a silver coin. He thanked Ossian kindly for his company, as though he were a stranger.

"Will they blame you for Scrope's death?" Ossian asked him.

Adam shook his head slowly. "Not if they can take Hungerford himself. And Scrope, I think, may have been a bait to draw Hungerford in. I heard a whisper that the bait was taken. These are cruel men, Ossian, not fools. They may need me again."

The loss of the elixir upset Adam far more. He spent hours poring through the sad detritus of his experiments. All must be fresh begun, all the apparatus repaired and purified. The authorities on whom Adam most relied – Jabir, Albertus Magnus, his beloved Doctor Bacon – were eagerly reread and the errors of their followers scorned in quiet, bitter words. And still there was something missing – some last, decisive step Adam hesitated to take.

Ossian had seldom seen hesitation in his master. By that he knew the step was a forbidden one.

OSSIAN HAD TAKEN *Death of a Mayfly* to the garden to read. He wanted to be able to say he had finished it when he wrote Lizzy that letter at last, but the sun was far too bright, the book a little too heavy to be comfortable. Instead, he laid it over his face and let the words seep through the skin of his closed eyes.

The dinner gong awoke him suddenly and sent the Gordius book splashing to the grass. He slid out of his seat and went into the house. As he reached the saloon, he was aware of someone close beside him.

*"She's made a start then?"*

It was Colin's voice, just by his ear.

"Pardon me?" said Ossian.

"My sister. Don't pretend you don't know what I mean! She's good, isn't she?"

Ossian recovered himself. "At croquet? Yes, very – thrashed me."

Colin laughed. "And after? Perhaps she offered to help you improve the grip on your mallet?"

Ossian turned slowly and stood to face Colin nose to nose. Or nose to forehead – he was a good half-head taller than Colin these days, and fitter too. It pleased him to see Colin flinch slightly. "What's that supposed to mean?"

Colin made a rough, throat-clearing noise. "Our Sue has a good eye, I'll give her that. And now, I bet, you can't get her out of your head. I've seen it all before."

"What's it to you?" said Ossian.

"There's no mystery," smiled Colin. "Sue has a way of getting under people's skin. Her methods can be pretty brutal. I warned you, didn't I? You can't pretend I didn't."

Colin's face wasn't cherubic any more, not like when they were kids. He looked as shifty as a puddle slicked with oil. Ossian didn't know what to make of him.

"Just back off," Ossian said as they went through the French windows to where dinner was laid out on the patio. "I can look after myself, you know."

He wondered if he sounded as if he meant it.

Jack and Catherine were in high spirits over soup. They were planning a trip up the valley, in search of views of sky and chalk, and whatever it was that had hung such a subtle green veil over this part of England.

"You ask why I don't paint portraits any more?" Jack was saying. "But I do! The landscape is a vast and *intimate* portrait of the people who inhabit it. That's what I missed in America. They had geology there, not landscape. Without history, a rock is a rock is a rock. When I came back, I understood that more clearly than ever."

Mr Frazer, from the way he was murdering his breadstick, was clearly finding Jack's rhapsody an irritation. Now he saw his chance to pounce. "And yet this morning you were objecting to the marina project precisely because it would disturb an unspoiled coastline. So which do you want, Jack? A garden or a wilderness? Get your story straight."

"It's a question of scale," said Jack, adroitly shifting ground. "You can't turn the entire south coast into a garage forecourt. It is possible to work in harmony with the surroundings."

"Harmony!" grunted Mr Frazer, turning the word into an exasperated cough. "Don't give me that eco-cant, Jack. We don't live in one of your watercolours."

"That's hardly what I meant," rejoined Jack wearily, but not as if he cared much either way. Ossian could tell from his glassy look that in spirit his father was already back in the rented two-seater scorching a line up the valley and startling sheep. And that in this fantasy Catherine was at his side.

"So, Cathy, are you still up for our little spree?"

Here we go again, Ossian thought. Can't resist, can he? Doesn't he see Frazer's about to lose it?

As soon as he was able, Ossian used the pretext of clearing plates to follow Sue to the kitchen. He was promptly issued with a dishcloth.

"I've wondered sometimes," he said experimentally, once the housekeeper had left the room, "if there wasn't something going on between my dad and Cathy once. Last time we were here."

Sue snorted. "In his dreams maybe!"

Ossian hadn't expected that. His pride was a little hurt on his father's behalf.

"Why not?" he protested. "She wouldn't be the first. There's something about being an artist, you know—"

"Ha! The agony and the ecstasy? Yes, I know all about them. We've had our share of both over the years, with Mum's pets. Half the time they're begging for handouts and the rest they want you to worship them as a kind of superior being. Mum's not as easily impressed as she used to be. Even seven years ago she had your dad's measure. Let's face it, Ossian – he's got talent, but he was never the hottest property around."

Sue went to the cupboard to put away some plates.

"Besides," she added haughtily over her shoulder,

"what makes you imagine Mum would ever be unfaithful to my father?"

That scruple had not even occurred to Ossian. Mr Frazer – he of the shiny pate and vintage clarets – was seldom to be seen except at dinner, when his conversation revolved around flotations and foreign exchanges, shares and bonds. In his other incarnation, he was the King of the Hedge, a topiary sculptor in braces and floppy hat. Ossian had barely registered his existence. Except that now his was the loudest of the raised voices on the patio. He and Jack were rowing again, this time about chemical fertilisers.

Sue, meanwhile, had raced ahead of him. "For Mum and your dad, you should perhaps read..." stretching for a top shelf "...you and me."

"What?"

"You're never too young to learn. You were besotted with me the first time you came here."

"Now, come on—" Ossian grinned, but his eyes registered a strange dismay.

"Quite a crush you had on me. Don't tell me you've forgotten? Fickle boy!"

She was teasing him. Behind the teasing words Sue's porcelain face was inscrutable. Ossian had no memory of a crush – hardly any memory of Sue at all. But it was a long time ago. There had been many girls since then. Debbie Candarino, for instance, and Emma Lomax. Lizzy!

Though Lizzy was much more than a crush, of course.

"I sometimes think," said Sue in an abruptly melancholy and reflective way, "that you fall in love properly just once in your life. And that's the first time. Everything else is just an echo. Variations on that theme."

"Is there any more washing-up liquid?" Ossian asked.

"And if that's true," she continued dreamily, "then wherever you go, Ossian, and whoever you meet, you'll always really be in love with me. In the corner cupboard, behind the scouring pads. Because I'm your one and only. And that, I'm sure, will be a great comfort to us both."

LIZZY.

LIZZY. LIZZY. LIZZY. LIZZY. God knows what she'd say about it all.

And he *still* owed her a letter.

Ossian had been meaning to write to Lizzy for days – ever since that first, abandoned attempt. He'd promised to write as soon as he got to England and had miserably failed. He'd set aside hours, whole afternoons, for the purpose. But something had always held him back until he was too tired and hot to think of what he ought to say. He'd been carrying around that duty gracelessly, pushing it to the side of each day's plate like an overboiled sprout. And the longer he left it, the more unappetising it became. How could he explain why he had not written in three long days?

"Don't forget me, will you?" she had said.

It was Sue's fault, of course. He was angry with Sue – angry for making him like her, just to show she could. And that nonsense about the Corn Stone was nothing but a new move in the game she was playing with him, a new way of landing him in the shrubbery. But he'd had enough. He was going to write Lizzy that letter – that long, proper letter – now.

He bounded up the stairs to his room, took out his good pen and the sheets of Lychfont writing paper. *Dear Lizzy*, he wrote. *You won't believe how much I miss you...*

But now he found that something strange had happened. The more he thought of Lizzy, the less he could remember. For nine months they had been together almost every day. Jack had been out of the way, capturing the Pennsylvania scenery. Nine intimate, joyful months – and what memories had he got to show for them? One or two crept back, grudgingly. That trip to the races, for instance.

He'd won 300 dollars and whooped down the street like a bank-breaking millionaire. She had made a paper crown and dubbed him King of Philadelphia Park.

He clutched the memory like a prize. That much, at least, was certain.

Or was it? Hadn't that happened to someone else, in fact? Wasn't it a scene from one of the short stories Lizzy kept trying to get published? He tried to remember her voice and found her phrases running through his mind like water, beyond recall.

"Come back, won't you?"

"Do you love me, errant boy?"

"I think you'll never understand me."

His pen hung drably over the paper:

*Oh, Lizzy, how I wish I'd never left...*

THE BRAZEN HEAD was proving troublesome. Obtaining the raw materials had been hard enough – gruesome, even. Sulis had not been able to watch at times. But there had been a kind of fascination in seeing the scryer work. He was undoubtedly a craftsman and Sulis appreciated all displays of skill. He had made the cast cunningly with earth, oil and tight-packed plaster. He had painted the metal nose and cheeks, given it ruby lips and jet-black hair (which echoed hollowly when tapped with Sulis's ivory wand), then set it securely on a wooden platform. Since he had brought the Head back to Sulis's kitchen at Lychfont, however, his plan had faltered.

Very ceremoniously, the scryer lit a green fire under its neck. A slow hiss of sandalwood scented the room. At last, the metal became scalding to the touch and smoke streamed from the eye holes.

"Pretty," said Sulis. She sat in a robe, sniffing. The smoke of the sandalwood made her eyes stream. But the Head's resemblance to her lost Ossian threatened to draw forth true tears. How could love and hate exist in such proximity? Her fate – hers and Ossian's – were tragically entwined, to be sure. The faithless wretch!

The scryer smiled indulgently at his patroness. "Your sympathy, madam, will surely draw the loved one to you," he said tactfully. Quite different from the crisp voice he used now, turning to his creation.

"Who is your master?" he demanded of the Brazen Head.

No answer came at first. The scryer stood in uncertainty. His face reddened. Then, at last, a faint voice echoed, from somewhere deep down and far away. Rapidly the sound grew louder and harder, as if hurtling upward through a long brass tunnel, and at length it issued from the red lips of the Head:

**"YOU ARE MY MASTER!"** it clanged.

The scryer smiled. "That is good. I command you then to tell me the truth. But a little more quietly, please. Where may we find the man we seek?"

After some more gargling, the Head mumbled: **"I do not understand."**

"Where is Ossian?"

**"OSSIAN! OSSIAN! OSSIAN! OSSIAN! OSSIAN!"** the Head repeated, beating out the name again and again like a flail.

"That's a great help!" sneered Sulis. The scryer gave the Head a blow with the flat side of his stick. The noise abruptly ceased.

The scryer grunted. "Let's try another approach. Head, what is the scope of your knowledge?"

No answer.

"Do your powers end suddenly or with a gradual diminution over space or time?"

**"I know that, but I will not tell you,"** declared the Head firmly.

"Who does it think it is?" cried Sulis.

"No cause for alarm, lady. Some reluctance is only to be expected." Nevertheless, it was with a degree of exasperation that he asked: "Head, is there some boon you would ask of us?"

"**To outlive a mayfly,**" echoed the Brazen Head.

"I suppose that passes for humour in the land of the dead," said Sulis. She turned impatiently to the scryer. "This Head of yours is impertinent. And totally unhelpful, which is worse."

The scryer hit the obstreperous Head again.

"Ingrate! I gave you life!"

"**Gaaaaarn!**" The Head groaned – a rasp of metal on metal, deep within its brazen skull. "**1—1— 1—1—1—1!**"

"And now it's playing for sympathy!"

"Quiet!" hissed the scryer. He motioned her away distractedly. Sulis snorted, but complied. She paced the room a while, then stepped outside and took her favourite walk, where the osiers, twisted with clematis and honeysuckle, shaded her and the camomile sprang underfoot all the way to the river's edge. There was her island with its little tower, delightful. She would rest there a while, until the scryer's task was done. The part she had played in acquiring the Head had not been a pleasant one and she wished to put the memory of it from her for a time.

In truth, she had also tired of the scryer's company and conversation. His words grated on her no less than those of his ridiculous Head. Before. After. Then. Now. Cause. Effect. Her own head quite spun with it all. To think in such narrow terms was surely unnatural, a thinning somehow of the true richness of things, a wretched truncation, a sad—

She hesitated. What was the word the scryer had used? *Impoverishment.* Yes, that described it rather well. A sad impoverishment. But why had Ossian preferred a life of deceiving shadows to one of infinite clarity – with her? It made no sense, or sense only of the most ghastly and perverted kind. It was with great difficulty that she forced herself to face the question.

*Could he really have ceased to love her?*

She climbed the tower nimbly. Never. He never could, not him. Never, never, never.

This was as close as Sulis ever came to pondering her own feelings. For her, self-knowledge was as free and open as the air. Wisdom was simply another word for her own actions and their results. She had her secrets, yes, and sacred mysteries; but she had no landscape of the mind and needed none, her nature being so perfectly expressed in this estate of Lychfont. That was why Ossian's crime could not be overlooked. Then or now, here or elsewhere,

Ossian was part of that landscape, part of Sulis herself. She could hardly believe that the scryer did not understand all this instinctively.

In her tower she lay with her face to the sun. She dreamt, indeed, of Ossian as she loved to think of him, ardent and rosy-cheeked, fresh from the hunt. She was in love and trying so hard to make him love her back, planting sweet kisses on his tender neck. He struggled and twisted but relented at the last... Sweet victory! She smiled as she dreamt of it.

When Alaris came to tell her mistress that the Head had revealed Ossian's first and last hiding place, she found Sulis already asleep and murmuring his name. Alaris turned discreetly and made her way back down the willow ladder. She would not for all the world have waked her.

# THREE

OSSIAN HAD BEEN proud to go on that journey. It was not for everyone to take. All in white, he stood in the coracle, the boatman before him, the priest his father at his back. The others were already on the island, coaxing the fire. The land rippled slightly as they crossed the running current, but Ossian did not sit. He stood astride the vessel – vibrant, alert.

It pleased him to think of his envious friends, back in the village. They could see him from its outskirts, if they climbed the Stone of Cernunnos. Madoc and Beli, they might dare. Seth would not. She feared the Stone. The boat ran into the soft island mud. Ropes and poles were hauling it ashore, while an elder handed Ossian's father to the loose shingle. A path had been worn through the undergrowth. The trees grew thick at the top of the bank, impenetrable except where the osier branches had been stripped of their green and twined into a low arch. Ossian bowed and entered.

Beyond the archway a grass track looped the island. It was some ten paces wide at its broadest – edged by the water and a flimsy inner fence of rushes. Ossian dawdled beside a small hut where his father stored the implements of leather, gold and bronze. The old man lifted the curtain and let him touch them: the torques, the sacerdotal flail, the Cup of Potencies. Ossian was awed, but puzzled too. He had expected to find more, remembering the war booty that had made its way to the island over the years. The weapons and brooches were sacred to the river – but surely the goddess would keep something back for herself? He supposed they were piled inside that rush fence.

The priest admonished him: "You are honoured. The goddess has shown you special favour or I would not have brought you here for another year at least. Acknowledge that with your behaviour. Be brave, devout and pleasant."

"Father, I will."

His father went to talk with the three novices whose birth and prowess had fitted them to Sulis's service. The young men huddled by the fence of rushes, fearful of what might lie inside. Ossian was still just too young for that.

Another blessing; he had no wish yet to meet the goddess face to face. He explored the island instead. It took no more than five minutes. At its far end, where the river met itself again and spun off to the sea, a pair of swans was nesting. They ignored him until he approached the nest too close, and then hissed and chased with their arm-thick necks thrust forward. Hastily, he returned to the inlet where he had disembarked. He looked at the fence of rushes once again. There was no one about. The novices would be inside by now, his father too. The latch was loose on the nearest gate. He put out his hand to loosen it further, when—

"Ahh!"

Across the back of his hand was a track of white flesh, red-beaded where his father's flail had caught.

"That is the holy place!" said his father. He was hoarse with anger and fear. "Not for you!"

"I only wanted to see—" Ossian began, eyes welling.

"Your fingers are dung! Your eyes would pollute her!"

He left Ossian sobbing at the doorway.

Minutes later his father returned and found the rag of a boy crouched under the sharp alders. The goddess had pitied him, he said. He kissed Ossian and forgave him, and gained his fervent promise never to enter the enclosure until he should be called there.

"When you will be a wise and powerful priest. So my stones tell me."

But later, when the sun's fire dimmed and midges were dancing on the river, when the trout had risen and the wind was sifting the willows' thinness – then Ossian heard her small cloaked voice. No larger than a chestnut bud, than his own heartbeat – it cried out, desolate:

"Husband! Lover!"

He ran back to the rush fence. It looked flimsy. Each year that fence had to be renewed – his father's task. They could have built a temple of stone, his father had told him, but a goddess should not need stone to guard her holy place. It would shame her people. That was why they left the spoils of war to the rain and crows, free for all to see. No one would touch them; their piety was protection enough. Pity the foreign gods, his father would say. Pity the gods of the south, with their temples of iron and marble. Sulis's weakness is more mighty than their strength.

But she had called him from within the fence.

"Husband! Brother!"

There was no mistake. Sulis – yes! *his* Sulis – was afraid.

He did not wait. His body was strong and the goddess had called only to him. Her light shone at his brow, danced like the river midges. He was transfigured, tall. In that moment he remembered whose consort he was and what feats were his to perform. He could vault that fence to save her. He could pull the sky down upon her enemies, throw stars like slingshot. He was Cynan and Bel and Bran. He could, could...

...could nothing. The light at his brow faded and left him Ossian again, cold and small on the midge-ridden island.

He skulked to the gate where the latch was still loose. There was no guard, for Sulis's sanctity should require none. But there were people. He knew their voices, and he knew the sticky smell of pitch, and the torchlight.

He bent and crooked his face to see inside.

THE SUN, RISEN not so long ago, had laid the chimneys of Lychfont down in damp plaits of shadow across the grass. Jack Purdey was sketching at his balcony, using charcoal and rough paper to put leaves on trees, deck hedges and plant swans on the just-visible water. He worked fast to catch the light in each of its gradations, grasped like a child at the lifting of each veil. There was no noise of traffic and the lawn's dew was undisturbed, but a digger chugged in the distance and its gear-changes reached him in chesty splutters of effort. Jack pursed his lip. The machine was spoiling his concentration. Probably something to do with that damned marina, he decided.

Below him, on the patio, there was no one. Only the echoes of last night's conversation swirled between the legs of chairs and tables, blown with the rest of that day's litter. Once or twice he started at the sound of stifled laughter. Once or twice he sighed.

So much for *The Golden Age*, he thought wryly. He did not think they would be staying in Lychfont very long. Cathy's idiot of a husband had made that plain last night. Jack groaned. Organo-phosphates! What a thing to have a stand-up row about! But he was not going to sneak away like some chastised schoolboy. As if he were ashamed. He was not – he was quietly angry, that was all, and his exit would be dignified.

Now he was distracted too, because he had just spotted Ossian at the edge of the lawn, walking very determinedly towards the woods. He was carrying his good camera with the telephoto lens – a sure sign he would not reappear for several hours. Wriggling out of being a shepherd again, thought Jack with slight irritation. Not that it mattered now. There were too many egos in this Arcadia. His commission would never be completed. He returned to his sketch. And –

funny! There was Colin too. Colin was following Ossian, but at a distance and furtively, as if he did not want to be seen. Jack was an inquisitive man and would normally have found all this intriguing. Today they were spoiling his landscape. Oh, well, they're gone now, he consoled himself as Colin disappeared amongst the trees. No great harm done, except—

Hmm, thought Jack fastidiously. Those boys have left their footprints in my dew.

"I WARNED YOU not to enter here! Was my meaning not plain?"

"But, master, he brought a warrant!"

Adam turned from his work in annoyance. Though he had not bolted the workshop door, his instructions had been clear. He was to be left alone with his books and equipment. He could not be disturbed in this most delicate work.

It had been that way ever since the death of Scrope. The loss of the elixir had shaken him – but there was more to it than the ruin of one experiment. Adam's work had taken a new and secret turn, perhaps a dangerous one, and

Ossian was not invited to his counsels. The room was shuttered, with only a candle's shady glitter to light it. There Adam kept all the instruments needed for the union of the Red King and White Queen, for alchemy's great marriage. Ossian had expected to find a maze of glass and liquid, of calcified powders and subtle, sponged chambers, a den of steam and delicate stored fire.

Instead, he blinked. At first, he did not know what it was he saw.

The woman on the table was not quite dead. Her left hand, dangling, gripped and released a loop of embroidered stuff, brown with blood. Her fingers too were freaked with brown where the skin creased, but the bleeding was old. Ossian could not see her face, which overhung the table edge so that she must lift her head to breathe freely. Too weak for that, she hardly breathed at all. Adam was turning a tight strip of linen around her other arm, the one Ossian could not see.

Her one shoe was awry – a rough leather sandal patterned with waves – and Ossian straightened it. Then he handed Adam a sealed note.

"Who gave you this?"

"The messenger who brought you to Scrope," said Ossian, gathering himself. "He's gathered a harvest of smiles. Says he will wait for your answer."

Adam looked down at the paper, frowning. The hand was strange to him. He feared the subtlety of these clerkish men. They knew too well how to express themselves in a double sense. He must be careful, lest one of those fine flourishes or hanging loops slip tight about his own neck.

"I must have this interpreted. Our fine messenger – where is he?"

"He waits above, master. Shall I send for him?"

"No, I'll go. I need to see his eyes. You stay with this one." He strode briskly to the door, then turned. "Do not speak to her," he said.

As Adam left he wiped his hands clean on his shirt, a quick fussy gesture. After the slam of the door came footsteps, the scrape of metal, the titter of conversation on the floor above. And the woman who was not quite dead said: "Ossian!"

Ossian started in fear. Adam had surely not mentioned his name in her hearing? But "Ossian!" she was calling again, not so loud but more urgent, and the syllables barbed and caught and drew him to her, to the face he had not yet looked upon, that was turning to him only now.

The woman was a girl. How pale she looked! Her eyelids were blue as lead. A clean incision ran two inches from her wrist towards her elbow, and was held open with a clamp and leather wedges. All the layers of her flesh were visible, clear as sediments in an earth bank. The wound still bled but, thanks to the linen strip tied about her upper arm, no longer freely. Ossian doubted she had much blood left to give, judging by the basin at his feet. He had never seen skin so waxen, death-like, perfect. He would hardly have known her.

But the girl was not quite dead.

"Ossian, you fool," she said, "you got here at last."

A look of contemptuous affection lit her face faintly.

"How could you let things come to this...?"

She seemed to be wrenching the effort to say something more, but could manage no better word than "fool" again. "You fool. Fool."

"It was you," mumbled Ossian. "You're the girl I saw at the ford."

The girl closed her eyes in exhaustion.

"Are you a witch?" Ossian asked recklessly. "Master Price has said..."

Her eyes flickered a little. "Master Price? Ask him, up in the room above. Ask what he wanted of me. A spirit to smoke out the elixir, that was his ransom. He took me for the Devil's hedge-child."

"Who brought you to him? Was it the Abbot? What are you charged with?"

"No one brought me, Ossian," she sighed. "Adam Price himself. He's been watching my house and says – don't ask how – I summoned demons. He'll swear to the Abbot that he saw me linking arms with Lucifer."

She did not seem to care if he believed her. That made Ossian want to know. Her white face could not be read.

"Is that the truth? Are you a witch? Did you send a spirit to protect me that day?"

The girl groaned. "You are the kind who hears a raven croak and thinks he has met the Devil. Look at my eyes, Ossian."

Ossian looked. Her eyes, green-blue jade, shone from the white face and trapped his own. He was looking at himself.

"Susannah?" The name tripped and fell from his mouth. He did not know where it had come from.

"You see? You know my name. Now who is the witch, my brother?"

"I'm not your brother!"

"If you doubt that, turn and go. But my mother told me how she wrapped a two-legged bundle once and left it at the door of Adam Price. One of us she could barely raise, not both – it was beyond her. She was not strong."

The voices in the room above were louder now. Adam was haggling, pretending not to know his own mind.

"I didn't know," said Ossian, in a whisper.

"Now, consider. Are you content to see your sister butchered before your eyes? To hold the basin even, to catch her blood like any slave?"

The witch's eyes did not blink, but Ossian saw them narrow, then the light that had seemed to lock his own gaze dulled a little. Even now, Ossian did not look away. Her words filled his mind and they were truth. He could not doubt them. Here was his sister, a fragment of himself. Now, he saw clearly, only now, how maimed a soul he had always carried. Adam Price his maker? In his own grim image? That was lies, all deception. Without Susannah, Ossian was just a fragment of a boy.

It was witchcraft, no doubt. How else could fifteen years of Adam Price's care and vigilance have been so suddenly overturned? As if Adam had been no more than a chance stranger and not – as Ossian knew him to be – an honest Christian, his own thousand-fold benefactor. Adam had given him everything: meals and shelter, care in sickness, the apprenticeship itself. His own son's portion, had he had a son. Only sorcery could have made Ossian cast him off so abruptly.

But now he was with Susannah and she was his poor sister.

"Where is our mother?" he asked.

"Dead."

"Can I see her grave? Where is she buried?"

"It's nothing but a piece of ground. Far away. You tire me," said the blue lips, "Ossian."

"Where is she? If you are my sister – I don't even know her name."

"Fool. She's sailed far off..."

Ossian clenched his fist. "Tell! Or I'll—"

"She's buried by the crossroads, torturer's boy! Murdered by one of your master's canting priests." Her eyes spiked him. "You'll not ask me why? For finding stolen gold with a raven's feather. A chalice lost from the Lady Chapel. She traced it with a bright black feather and some smoky words and six grains of good wit. *She* didn't need to torture any living soul. And when she asked for her reward, they said: 'You may choose. Will you be hanged as a thief or a witch?'"

Susannah turned her head aside. Her story had exhausted her and Ossian saw she would not speak again. Perhaps she would never speak, unless he could move her from this place.

But that was impossible. Her body was clamped and strapped. Besides, she was too weak; even the attempt might kill her. And now Adam's boots were heavy on the stairway and Adam would know at once that they had spoken.

Ossian couldn't lie to Adam – not with words. Even his eyes might betray him. Adam Price had chiselled out every reflex in his body, had he not? With relentless care and watchfulness. How could he fail to guess his mind?

The door opened and Adam came in looking pleased. His shadow filled the doorway, but his eyes were bright. "Fetch your dancing shoes, Ossian. Tomorrow we must play before the Sheriff himself."

He threw Ossian a coin. Ossian bit and tasted gold.

"A token of his lordship's goodwill," said Adam. "Master Blackthorn would have kept it as the price of his errand, but I persuaded him to honesty." He opened his broad palm for the coin's return and Ossian thought, as he laid it on the dark-stained flesh, how very persuasive Adam Price could be. Even so, he knew he was lucky. Had Adam not been distracted he would certainly have noticed the fear in Ossian's own face or the tremor of his fingers as their hands touched.

"Sleep, Ossian," was all he said. "Tomorrow we must ride to Winchester and teach Lord Hungerford himself to sing in tune."

Susannah was groaning low, too far gone to hear them.

"What about her?" asked Ossian. "What is she?"

"My business. Sleep now, Ossian. I'll patch her and Mother Bungay will have the care of her while we're away.

So – to your bed. I'll make things ready here, lay out our tools and damp the fire down."

OSSIAN HAD STALKED the marsh beds much of the morning. Snipe were rare in summer, but he had heard of a pair in the patches of wet heath between the Abbey ruins and the Solent. So he had taken his camera along the devious woodland paths behind the house and waited. He had seen squirrels, magpies, pigeons. A hectoring mallard splashed cumbrously into the peaty water and out again. And always Mr Frazer's dredgers were wrenching mud from the land's flank somewhere to the south, their engines' roar carried on the breeze.

Meanwhile, the letter to Lizzy lay abandoned on the desk in his room. He had decided now to leave that task until they were out of Lychfont. The place smothered his thoughts whenever he tried to turn his mind Lizzy's way – like a radio blind spot. It was strange, though there were no prizes for guessing the reason. He'd dreamt of Sue all of last night – hot, clammy dreams mostly, from which he'd woken in a froth of sweat and hair. Except for the last one. In that he'd been walking the banks of a shallow, black lake, its border clogged with yellow sedge. His legs hurt and all the time a high, midge-buzzing whine sounded in his ears, and the more he tried not to listen, the more it sounded like a voice from the lake's heart.

"Husband! Come quickly!"

He shook his head; even by daylight that whining still seemed to be with him. It had blended with the sound of the dredgers and the songbirds' twitter, the taut hum of the summer light itself.

Ossian packed up his equipment and wandered. Almost at once he found his path crossed by a serpentine inlet of the Solent. Here was a small landing stage: the Frazers' old jetty. He smiled, surprised by another memory. Wasn't this where they had sat and plotted in the old days – him and Colin? It was a secluded place, still rural despite the yachts and ferries nearby. Southampton might as well not exist. Low tide, however, had revealed an urban beach strewn with tyres and plastic bottles. The cracked ribs of a cabin cruiser curved under his feet.

He did not linger there. He threaded the maze of willow and alder, climbed the tree roots up an earth bank and looked down the ditch on its far side. The ditch-bottom was still muddy, a ferment of leaf litter, just as it had been in the days when Colin had sent him to capture toads there. Colin had worked dry-shod, picking off green twigs from the overhanging trees to make a wreath of willow. From here they had walked to the Corn Stone, where Colin laid down his offering solemnly, while Ossian let the dazed toad hop from his hand.

"Accept our offering, oh God of the Stone," Colin had said in a hollow voice. He had brought a heavy, jagged rock with him. They looked down at the yellowy-brown quiver of flesh. It had reminded Ossian of a plant more than an animal, some rare fungus he had tusked out like a rooting pig.

"Kill it then, Ossian!" said Colin, handing him the rock at the last moment. "Smash its head!"

Ossian smashed it. He brought the rock down once – twice. The fungus was a splay of innards and split flesh, bone and brain froth. The head was gone. Only one foreleg had survived, by chance, without injury.

Colin stood there, disapproving. "You did it wrong! You should have killed it with one blow!"

"But – but it's dead," Ossian stammered.

"No good!" said Colin coldly. "It was spoiled! Now its spirit will be hungry..."

That was a long time ago. Now Ossian was standing on the same earth bank, facing out towards the Solent. The sun had scattered sequins of angled light across the distant water. Would that make a good shot, he wondered? He experimented with the camera zoom for a while before deciding that it would not. It was all to do with time, that effect – not space. The light would not pose for him and he didn't know how to fake it. Turning inland, he raised the camera again – and saw a rushing green blur at first, so close he was forced to steady himself. He gasped. The colour broke on him with the force of a wave, setting him adrift in a sea of greenness. Then he realised that he was seeing nothing but the top of the nearby alder tree, enlarged and out of focus. He adjusted the camera and the blur resolved into veined leaves and twigs, and a wood pigeon. The bird was preening itself. It dug its beak in under the feathers of its wing obliviously. Watching, Ossian experienced a strange sensation of power. To be so close and not be known! He trained the camera lower, to the reed-spiked ditch that ran the edge of the field. He tracked slowly along it, then climbed a bank of daisies, up to the field where the Corn Stone sat.

He stopped. The Stone was different. A tartan blanket was spread out on the grass next to it. He took the camera away, wanting to check what he was seeing with his own eyes.

Sue Frazer lay beside the Corn Stone. She was sunbathing in a pale green bikini. The music – Ossian realised he had been hearing music for the last few minutes – must be coming from that radio beside her head. He pursed his lips, feeling obscurely cheated. He realised now that this was where he had been meaning to arrive all morning. He had not come to photograph wildlife but to visit the Corn Stone – to compare the reality of it with Sue's weird theories and prove her wrong. But that he couldn't do if Sue was here first. He felt annoyed, unreasonably so. It was as if she *knew*.

Ossian looked through the zoom again, experimentally. Again he was unprepared for the sudden obliteration of distance. His gaze was buried in Sue's flesh and the closeness of her body astonished him. Each nail, each nostril and lock of hair imprinted itself on him as if he had been made of wax. The sun was at his back and in the oblique light Sue's skin seemed made to dazzle – a blazing paper-white.

There was no birdsong. The only sound was the music from the radio by Sue's head: a chiming ripple of bells and a ragged chorus that made him half afraid, though the words were bland enough:

*Two-timer, you ran out on me*
*But if you come back now*
*I'll show you how*
*To make it good*
*Sooo good*
*I'll show you how to love me.*

Sue was sitting up now, and the sun was glinting on her face as if on polished glass. Ossian realised with astonishment that she was weeping! Her face was wet with tears! She had turned his way, her long legs stretched out towards him. Ossian panicked. If he moved now, he would surely be seen. But no, she was beyond noticing anything but her own tears and the shallow melancholy of the song she played.

What could be the matter with her? Sue's tears seeped through her fingers and down her forearms, down to the white tips of her elbows, dripped and ran over her slim calves.

*You better believe it*
*You never should have gone...*

He let the camera drop about his neck and slid to the bottom of the bank, then squinted towards the Corn Stone again. It was blindingly bright, now, and it was some moments before he was able to make out objects clearly. He blinked. There was the tartan rug and the little radio. A streak of white, just in front of the rug, revealed itself as a bunch of daisy heads. And the radio song jangled on:

> *...and you'll be sorry!*
> *Sooo sorry*
> *When I show you how to love me.*

But of Sue Frazer herself there was now no sign at all.

"WHEN THEY CAME to the tree it was aflame with red and yellow fire, you see? And in all that brightness it was a hard thing to spy the raven sitting in the topmost branch, and harder still to throw a spear that would shave its wing and make it fall down to sit on a man's fist."

Ossian paused. The little ones looked up at him, waiting. They wanted to know what happened next – the secret it was his to give or keep. They dared not break the spell by asking.

He smiled generously. "That raven granted wishes," he explained. "That is how my father became a wise man. His brothers asked for gold and weapons; he asked for knowledge."

They had left the yard and come to sit in a secret patch of reed and sedge that could not be spied from the roundhouse. Ossian had avoided his father since his visit to the island and taken to playing with the younger children. He was ashamed of what his eyes might admit if his father searched there. Luckily, the old man was distracted with the quest for the Red King, the new Cernunnos. Half his days he was not even in the mortal world, but seeking Sulis through the broad meadows of her own country, bringing gifts to lay at her feet. Even so, Ossian needed to be careful and had made the company of children his refuge. He knew they admired him for his age and birth and he was happy there. But the knowledge had made him boastful.

"My father took me to her island. He will do again, when I'm older; then I'll be allowed to see the goddess. You know, Beli and Madoc, but these younger ones may not, that only her priest may see her plainly. I had to wait outside the sanctuary. But I could hear them."

"What did you mean then, when you told me that her face was pale?" asked Seth.

"It's a secret." Ossian looked round furtively, as if to check for spies. "The fence had a gap. I glimpsed her, no more. Only a glimpse."

The small children nodded. They had seen the island from the bank, with its fence of fresh woven rushes – a green, floating crown at the last river bend. You couldn't go there, of course, not unless you were a priest or the son of a priest, a warden or a ferryman, a bard or a smith or a king. But everyone knew that was where Sulis lived. Her sanctuary grew from the centre of the isle and shade from its long trails of leaf-beaded branch spread over the waters. You could not swim out to it, for the current was too fierce. If you tried, besides, your arms and feet would be seized from below and you would find yourself being dragged down into the river weed and drowned. Each year since Ossian could remember, two or three people had died that way. They had been killed and nothing had ever been found of them except their bones, kicked heedlessly ashore as shingle on the river bank.

"You know who Sulis is, of course," Ossian told the streak-faced tots and they nodded vigorously. Only Madoc did not nod, but smiled privately to himself. "Without her, we could not live by the river at all. The sea would flood in and drown our crops; the tides would refuse to turn."

Two of the children were whispering together. Ossian didn't like that; he was affronted.

"You there!" he cried. "What are you saying?"

"We only want to know, what did you see through the rushes? Did you see the Lady of the Alder? Or the Moon Lady?"

"I will not tell you that," said Ossian piously. "My tongue would shrivel inside my mouth if I told it."

Madoc laughed softly. He did not believe Ossian had seen anything at all.

"Take that back!"

Ossian was on top of him at once. He was only eight, this boy; he did not have the breath to shout, or to take back anything.

"You want me to toss your sniggering lungs to the river?"

"I didn't say—"

"*Do you?*"

"No." The boy sagged. He was no longer pushing Ossian off; he was as limp as a cut rope.

Ossian rolled off the lad, on to his back. At this angle he could just make out the martin's nest under the roundhouse eave. A bird was twitching out of it, ball-headed, sharp-beaked. Wonderfully quick, then stone-still – it would make you dizzy to watch him. Ossian had already forgotten his anger.

"What did you see?"

It was gentle Seth asking. Seth who wasn't clever, who lived on kindness and milk and spelt bread. She asked softly, as she asked everything. "Was she very lovely?"

Ossian had to shut his eyes to remember. The rushes had crossed his face with swart shadow. Cinders of light, a gnat-cluster of them, floated through the clack of knuckle-bones. His father had been scrying. The others – Halter, Anvil, Potter's Wheel – watched by the spitting flame, but their faces were closed and dumb. Only his father's ancient face moved to the bones' clatter, stirred words into the air, shaped the ash with his finger. On the distant bank the women were keening Cernunnos. His body is blown like thistledown, they cried. His limbs are scattered on the sea. Never again shall we see his bright and handsome face, who was once as generous as the May time...

Each year their grief was green as holly, fresh as the first snowfall, bitter as rue.

"Yes," said Ossian. His eyes opened in blank tranquillity. "She was very lovely."

"They're coming," said Beli's sister, who had shielded her eyes against the blink of light. And there were the three coracles shimmering back across the water, away from the island. The high trees spilt down sloughs of shadow and for part of their way the boats were bogged in it. Only Ossian's father was clear, all in white, and he was looking back the way they had come. The rest were busy with paddles or watching for snags on the water. But he sat facing that heap of earth and rush as if he could scarcely bear to leave it, or had abandoned there the thing he loved dearly. The island itself had never lain so grey and still.

By now, other people had joined the children on the bank. Men and women, waiting for the coracles. One, with a long pole, paddled into the shallows to help grapple the boats ashore. Ossian's father, at any rate, could no longer do such work himself, not at his age, being who he was. He faced the island, oblivious of the zigzag course of the coracle under him, the cross-stress of the ribbed current.

"The goddess has spoken to him," Ossian heard someone say. "He is not in his right mind."

The men handed him out of the boat and he staggered through the tall grass, his robe catching his foot. His eyes, when they fell on the villagers at last, were blind, callused with hard seeing.

"Where is my son?" he asked the rushes, and they whispered back reedy lies to him. "Is he here?"

Seth looked at Ossian expectantly. Why didn't he answer? Why didn't he kneel for his father's blessing?

Ossian's own eyes were vacant. The reeds had pleated the wind, doubled every sound and sent the old man back to the paddle splash of the river, calling Ossian.

Ossian got to his feet slowly. He rubbed his hand across Seth's hair, for luck or comfort. Then walked down the green bank where the people – there was a crowd now – parted to let him pass and find his father ankle-deep in river weed, there calling always for his son Ossian.

No one touched him as he passed.

He knelt in the water and asked for blessing. He placed the blind fingers on his own eyes, let their nails shock his flesh. On the Isle of Rushes the goddess of the river watched from her willow tower.

"Give me your blessing, father."

The old man quivered like a poplar and his lips were dewed.

"I – I can't."

It was less than half a whisper and everyone heard. The entire village was gathered behind Ossian now. The other two boats were landed and their oarsmen had set a tinder-fire of rumour. The smith's forge was silent. The people had run from hearths and yards, left fish to burn on the fire, the bucket to fall glittering at the spring. They stood mute as winter, as the leaf in the moment before its fall.

"She has taken my blessing from me. It is no longer mine. You saw her face, Ossian. You are Cernunnos."

Ossian did not understand at first. His father must be talking about his initiation, a year from now. He knew something of that ceremony; how antlers were fitted to the novice's brow and the juice of harsh berries pressed to his nose on a sponge of moss. He knew that one day he would be called to follow his father to that dream country. Why else had he been taken to the Isle of Rushes? And he had always been so apt – quick, yes, to see the pattern of the knuckles sprawled in the dust, even to guess the goddess's temper. Not the detail, of course, not the sacred days she set aside to sow and reap, her particular demands for fruit or flesh, fresh or charred: not her sudden, onerous generosities. The priest alone was able to read these. But her mood he could tell keenly. Until this moment he had always felt her goodwill. He had not earned it, any more than the ripe fruit that drips with mist earns its sweetness, but it had been there, and he had lived subtly, half-consciously on her favour. Until now, at the moment of its withdrawal.

He was alone, bolassed in straggles of weed, and his father was a fanatic stranger.

"The goddess spoke to me!" the old man was crying aloud, and he waved his staff to the sky and threw out arcs of spray from the river's skin. "Behold, here is Cernunnos!"

Ossian saw the stick flick overhead against a sky scored with strange runes of cloud. The old man was there, and a plunge of feet, and the slopping water filled his nostrils, for he was lying in the river now, pushed and jostled there. And he could no longer hear what his father was praying for; the water was roaring in his ears and the words were strange to him – an ecstatic gibber, beautiful and senseless as a lark's trill, hot words, there were no gaps, no breath, and his feet had been seized and there were hands under his shoulders taking him roughly and he knew the choice had fallen on him.

OSSIAN STOOD BESIDE the Corn Stone. He was trying to remember what the place had once meant to him. The top of it had been level with his shoulder then, a solid stone block, solitary in the weedy field. Colin had claimed to be able to see blue water from its top, but Ossian had never dared climb it. He ran his finger across the place where a name had once been carved, a maze of baffling grooves and ridges that flaked at his touch. They were fragile, but they must have lasted years – centuries. Yet the Stone, so Sue said, was older still.

He put his hand to its surface, feeling the gritty ridge against his skin. Just a stone after all. Oolitic limestone, he told himself, trying to feel scientific. And if anyone was ever sacrificed here... it was a long time ago. A rock is a rock is a rock.

But – where was Sue?

"Gotcha!"

Ice-cold water was suddenly pouring down the back of his neck. He whisked round. Sue leered at him, a frosted bottle of water in her hand.

"You gave me a heart attack!"

She must have been keeping her cool bag on the far side of the Stone, in the shade. Now she was swarming across the top, clearly delighted with herself. "Serves you right, interrupting my quality time like that."

Ossian flapped the water from his shirt. He peered at her face. "Are you all right, Sue?"

"Never better, thanks. Why?"

"I thought I saw – you look like you've been crying."

"I do? Oh." She wiped her cheek casually and laughed. "Just a stupid song – 'Two-timer' always gets to me – God knows why. Didn't you realise I was the sentimental type?"

She eased herself gracefully to the ground. Ossian watched the slight recoil of her breasts as she landed – so neat and trim and self-contained.

"Why are you sunbathing out here, anyway?" he asked. "There are plenty of lawns at the house."

"You're nosy today! I'm avoiding my mother, if you must know. You've seen how she likes me to do the hostess bit – pouring drinks and passing cheesy things on plates. Give me a break! This is supposed to be a holiday."

Sue looked sidelong at him, then bent down to get her clothes. Ossian followed the long curve of her ribs where her pale skin had been rubbed pink by the sun. The sight hit him like a furnace blast. He was dazed by it. In a place where smart answers were the only currency, he could do nothing but stare clownishly. And stare, until a cloud of gnats swam up before his eyes and he thought he was about to faint...

When the swarm cleared, Sue was vaguely indicating the Stone with her foot. "So this is where it happened?"

"Where what happened?" he managed to ask.

"Oh, you know. Your deeds of darkness. The Death of Jeremy Fisher."

"We were only kids and it's not like we murdered someone," muttered Ossian. "You read too many detective novels."

"Perhaps," acknowledged Sue, pulling on a shirt. "But I'm not really bothered about toads. It's you I'm interested in, in case you hadn't noticed." She spoke lower and more urgently: "I'm fascinated by this strange attraction you seem to have. For ghosts, I mean!" she added, seeing his face. "You know I've seen them, moping after you."

"Maybe I'm a novelty," Ossian muttered. "I suppose ghosts can get bored like anyone else."

"Rubbish! Listen, Ossian." Sue leaned towards him confidentially. "Listen. This is something I haven't even told Colin about."

Her eyes changed with the light from the emerald grass. They flashed turquoise.

"I'm flattered," said Ossian cautiously.

"You should be. When they look at you, Ossian – and don't deny it, because I know I'm right – they see someone like themselves. Up the Styx without a paddle." She waited for him to react. "Maybe you're a kind of amphibian after all. I think someone round here has mistaken you for a dead person – or someone who ought to be dead..."

Ossian trod water in the deep silence that followed this. Hold on, he told himself, and it will sound absurd, ridiculous.

"Want to tell me what you mean by that?" he said at last.

"It's just – a kind of warning, I suppose," said Sue meekly. "But a useless one, because I don't know what you can do about it." She looked very serious. "I think you may be in danger here."

"Now I *know* you're overdoing the detective novels. You have suspects?"

"Far too many suspects and no crime as yet. People seem... nervous of you, hadn't you noticed? You make my mother jittery, that's a fact. I'll admit, even I – why, when I was holding that croquet mallet and you were groping around in the bushes for your lost shot, I felt a strange urge to knock a hole in your skull. Nothing personal."

Ossian gave a short laugh. "Course not!"

"I'd have been sorry to lose you, Ossian."

She smiled at him quite demurely – then caught the direction of his gaze, where her shirt was unbuttoned. He had been gawping, he realised. She shook her head a little, as if in disappointment, and stepped forward. And the scent was there again, encroaching subtly on his thoughts – not her coconut sun lotion but another smell, much more familiar though he could not place it. Leather was it? Charred wood? He remembered the way she had looked at him once or twice before, the tip of her tongue flicking and the turquoise eyes suddenly warm and hypnotic.

"Sue, wait!"

But Sue did not wait. She kissed him roughly. And he submitted as his body told him to and drew her close, and such was the rush of his desire that he did not even feel surprise at what was happening.

Then she had pulled away and was looking at him from just beyond an arm's length distant. Her expression was one of amusement, tinged with disdain.

"There," she said, slipping her sandals on. "That's all. You were wondering, weren't you? Now you know."

She regarded Ossian with a skewed smile. "Don't look so horrified, Ossian! You might stick if the wind changes. It wasn't so awful, was it? Look, bring in the cool bag for me, will you? I'm a bit laden."

Sue folded the tartan rug and set off across the field towards the house. Ossian tried to move his gaze away, but it was like pulling nails from a plank. Instead he leaned, winded, against the Corn Stone until she was out of sight. He groaned with shame and lust and with the humiliation of it all.

"Oh, Lizzy!" he said out loud.

He turned suddenly and punched his fist into the Corn Stone behind him. The shock of pain shot up his arm. His knuckles were bleeding, ugly rucks of thin white skin above the raw flesh. Good – he deserved it. Colin had warned him, after all. He should have listened to Colin.

He picked up Sue's cool bag and forced himself back towards the house as if he were dragging his own corpse. He watched the long grass bend and lie flat beneath his feet, and was aware of the flurry of legs and wings, the crushing of carapaced bodies and the sticky ruin of webs that accompanied his every step. But he did not look behind him until he came to the lawn again. If he had, he would have known that a furtive figure had followed him from the Corn Stone, that it had grown closer and more erect the nearer he came to the house, and that now it was just a few paces behind.

He glanced over his shoulder only when he saw the shadow dancing along the hedge to his right. He half expected to find a ghost there, but it was only Colin Frazer. Colin was looking pale and rumpled, as if he had not slept. When he saw that Ossian had spotted him, he attempted an upright swagger and sauntered up.

"Afternoon, Ossian," he said. "We need to talk."

OSSIAN HAD worked it all out – up to a point. He would slip away from Adam while he was questioning Lord Hungerford. He would retrace his steps from Winchester Castle and be back at Lychfont before Adam realised he was gone. Wait until Mother Bungay was out with her gossips and make Susannah safe in the cart. Though Susannah was weak, Adam had seen her wounds dressed and wholesome food provided for her before they left. Now, a week later, she might be fit to travel – a little way at least. But where could they go that Adam would not find them?

Ossian tried not to think about that question, because there was no answer to it. It conjured a fog in which he could see and hear nothing. Still, he had groped the outline of a plan. He would start for the next harbour down the coast. There a fisherman might be persuaded (Ossian had saved a little money) to give them shelter and, in due course, passage to another port. He would settle and learn a new trade. He warmed to the fantasy a little, picturing himself as... a carpenter perhaps. He had always been a quick hand at drawing and making, and with the right master he would do well. Susannah would grow strong again. No one need know she was his sister...

These thoughts were idle. Adam was too careful for that and knew him far too well. He would see each move in advance. Even the flight from Winchester was possible only because Adam was occupied as never before with this matter of Lord Hungerford. Hungerford was proving wilier than anyone had expected – wilier or braver or more stupid, and Adam complained that as yet it was hard to know which.

"But we'll smoke him out, Ossian; we'll smoke him. The truth may be beaten thin as air, yet still be golden."

Yes, the truth was elusive. The true reason Ossian did not wish to think about the future was that for Susannah there was none. She was dying, and all he hoped for was to have her die beside him, in his arms. He wanted her to know she had been loved.

He left Winchester in the hour before dawn, with the last stars guttering. The sky was written with small, curled clouds, gold like the parings Adam flaked off in his workshop and caught in a linen apron, their value was so great. Ossian took the main road. There were other ways, less public, he might have chosen, and there was light enough; but he knew it could not be long before Adam missed him – and Adam would be mounted. He was not sure of this country, besides. No, stick to the road you know, and hurry. Three miles, six, nine – across the striped fields and past the churchyards, through the hunting woods that grow thickest where the ground is too steep for the plough. A rich country, this – even the unplanted land is moist and black. A happy land – but watch for the eyes that watch you: deer, hawk, cony, fox. Avoid the charcoal burners' smoky ruin, the ancient ramparts topped with beech, the shaggy rook-filled trees. Pass quickly by Druid's Copse and find the river again, whose silver channels cross the road by bridge and ford a dozen times before they merge and flank it. Six, nine, twelve miles, and fifteen at last will crest the final hill and show you Lychfont Abbey, Dame of the Marshes.

The sun was high and unforgiving now. The shadows crouched under the eaves. Adam's house was easy to pick out, though, even if Ossian had to shield his eyes to do so. In the whole sweep of the sea-raked valley his was the only smoking chimney.

"God bless Mother Bungay!" cried Ossian as he set off down the hill.

God had blessed Mother Bungay. She was snoring, with a pitcher of ale at her side. Ossian sheathed his dagger and replaced the latch. He passed into the farther room, where Susannah was lodged. On a rush mat, under a woollen blanket, he found her. Heard her first – the rustling of her breath gave her away. Otherwise, she was still, appalling in her stillness. The place stank of Adam's experiments, and Ossian looked with new disgust at the vials of acidum salis and of vitriol, and the reeking jar of sheep's urine in which Adam hoped to steep a cross of copper and convert it, with Susannah's aid, to gold. Ossian spat. Who needed alchemy? He saw everything with transformed eyes now. He was himself converted. To Adam, Susannah was no more than an ingredient to be used and sluiced away. And this was the man to whom he owed his life? His Christian master? He steadied himself against the table.

"Ossian. I knew you'd come," she whispered.

"Don't talk." He was kneeling beside her. "I'm going to take you somewhere safe. Away."

"You have a winged horse in the yard?"

She laughed – horribly, painfully. But also loudly; Ossian clapped his hand over her mouth. "Mother Bungay!"

Susannah's eyes bulged with agonised laughter. "Ah, you really are the fool I took you for, sweet Ossian. She'd sleep through Doomsday now."

Ossian stared at her.

"Your master should never have tapped his beer so close under that jar of pretty green crystals."

It took a while for Ossian to understand. "You poisoned her?"

"I just made her – careless. Don't look so horrified! She did not change my dressings as Adam Price commanded her. She hit me and called me Satan's whore." Susannah's eyes blazed, challenging him to find fault in her. "She is a sloven," she added for good measure.

"But she'll wake again?"

"You ask too much. I am in pain now. Will you lift my shoulder, brother?"

Ossian fetched one of Mother Bungay's shawls. The snoring of Mother Bungay, he heard now, was not her own. It was a rattling, tongue-sucking snore that would have wakened her from any natural sleep. He did not want to listen to it. He feared that it would stop.

He cushioned Susannah's head with the shawl. The sacking beneath her dress was bloody, but the blood was old.

"I'll fetch Jerusalem," he said.

He put Jerusalem between the shafts, but it was pitifully hard, getting Susannah on to the cart. Every movement tore her wounds. He found a hurdle and pulled Susannah on to it, sacking bed and all. She whimpered like a child. Jolted over the threshold she screamed outright. And, having held her by the midriff to ease her in, he drew back his hand to find it scarlet with fresh blood.

"It's a corpse you'll be lugging to freedom," she whispered. "Fool."

Jerusalem did the lugging. Ossian was grateful that the weather had been dry for the past week. They left no tracks and the cart ran freely down the road from Adam Price's house to the river. But the hard ruts shook blood from Susannah at every step. Ossian guessed that it was eight hours since he had left Winchester. Adam must have noticed his absence. But perhaps he would not yet guess the reason for it. The night before, Ossian had been careful to speak of the fair at St Giles – a big place, full of booths and hawkers, and easy to get lost in. Adam would never have spared him, but Ossian had managed to sound wistful.

"They say there will be parrots, master."

So Adam might seek his errant boy with the parrots at St Giles Fair first, before he turned to Lychfont – and Ossian hoped for that. It was as close as he had ever come to telling Adam a lie.

He had covered Susannah with her blanket and a few scraps of sacking. But it was hard for her to stay silent as

Jerusalem pulled the cart along. At first they met no one. There were workers in the fields, but they were not interested enough in the distant sight of Ossian leading a cart to approach him. Adam's lad was tainted with Adam's own sinister power, an ill-omened child. It was only at the Kerney Stone that they found Peg of the Willow, the swaddling bundle at her breast, her with the ghosts for company.

"Where are you taking that dead lad, Ossian?" The question whistled out between her two good teeth. "What are you doing in a dead lad's skin?"

Peg was old – fifty years at least. Her baby son had died in her belly, and that was thirty years back. Being unbaptised, he could not be buried within the churchyard wall. But if he was not given a Christian burial, Peg demanded, then who was to say that he was truly dead? The priest, Sir John, grown gluttonous on tithes, could not answer her. Nor could Adam Price, the cunning man, for all his spells. They would hide it from her, but she knew the truth. Her William was alive. Or if he was not, he could be made to live, and she would make the necessary sacrifice. That was nothing but her mind, which she laid down willingly. William came to her now, in the shape of a raggedy moppet – and all other lads were dead lads next to him.

"I'm off to fetch firewood, Peg."

"There's wood in your barn. What do you need with firewood?" she asked.

"It must be the sweet-smelling pine that grows by the King's Wood. My master says."

"And why are you taking a dead lad with you?"

"There's no dead lad, Peg," said Ossian. He could not stop himself from glancing back to make sure that Susannah's legs were covered. The blanket trembled, a very little, with her breathing. "Just you and me."

"I can smell his sweet flesh from here. But Adam Price will have his secrets." She hugged the bundle to her and laughed.

Ossian slapped Jerusalem and they started off from the Kerney Stone. Peg of the Willow called after them. He heard the words again: "Dead lad!"

He turned back to Peg and made the sign against the evil eye. The laughter buzzed back down the slope from the Kerney Stone to the birch wood, through the grass where the track now took them. He could no longer make out Peg's voice. There was shelter here, a tunnel of leaning green with high banks. Ossian knew that it would guide them to a creek and so to a small harbour where two or three families kept their boats. They knew Ossian. He could have asked them for a roof that night for himself.

But for Susannah? He tried out lies in his mind until he found one that fitted. He would say he had found her robbed and wounded in the lane. If he could keep them from searching her wounds too closely, they would probably believe him. They must not see when those wounds had been made, nor how. He must not let them recognise Susannah as a witch's child.

"Stop!" said Susannah.

Her voice had been so faint that even the small sounds of the tunnel lane had swallowed it. Ossian abandoned Jerusalem and ran to the back of the cart. Susannah had somehow kicked her cover off. Her skin was mottled shadow under the restless leaves and, watching the play of the leaves on her skin, Ossian felt the lane change around him. It came to him that he was standing underwater, fathoms deep, that the lane was roofed with the green scum of a standing pool. Susannah's head was crooked, angled to the earth.

"What's wrong?"

Ossian's words bubbled from his mouth and pricked on the treetops.

"I've a pain. No, here." She placed his hand on her heart. "You're fading, Ossian."

Her lips barely moved. Ossian looked about him in panic. The lane was green, watery green, nothing but water. They were drowning in greenness. He had to get them away. Scrambling up through the trees at the side of the lane, he saw patchwork forest, then the river marshland: impassable, green. He fell back into the dyke lane and waded through green light to the other side, pulled himself up by green branches. First he saw only the dark mud floor split with leaf-light. A green, tranced world. Then: *dint, dint.* The blunt sound of a hammer on metal and there was a sign, nearby, of a broad red track and smoke at the end of it, and a warning voice told Ossian that there had been no forge in this place before. But the birds were spiralling from their roosts at the shunt of a hammer into red-hot iron, the whinny of a horse nervous at being shod.

There was Susannah dying at his back.

Ossian hurried to the cart. Jerusalem chewed a thistle, oblivious of the suffocating greenness in which he stood. Ossian urged the beast forward, to the dip in the bank where the red track split and curved between tall, spaced trees. Susannah said, did nothing. He was afraid that she was already dead and dared not look. The smithy was a low heap of mortared stone. The red path led straight to it and ended. There was no sign of the shod horse and the hammering died as they approached. Inside, though, someone was working a bellows. Ossian recognised the sound as it blew through the packed coals, turning them to dragon's teeth. Fire made him feel safe. He remembered – starved, gaunt days, with ice on the river and iron light, when Adam's fierce blaze had been his only comfort and he had clung to the hearthstones until he was cinder-black. He forgot to be careful about the cart and whipped at Jerusalem's flank to make him run.

"You'll be safe here," he heard himself say. "A smithy's safe."

The door of three lashed planks stood open. But the smell of the place was wrong. Not the leather and burned horsehair, the crimson-orange heat of the farrier; not the charred-bitter, metal-sour smell of the goldsmith's forge, but some yellow harsh poison, a sparking cloud of blue gases. And in the midst of that cloud sat Adam Price. He was pouring thick liquid from a glass vessel with a long swan neck. He looked up – but not in surprise – and, seeing Ossian, placed the vessel calmly on the table before him. Ossian recognised Adam's expression. It was the same one he had worn when he knew he would have to take the poker to Scrope's thigh.

"I am almost sorry," he said to Ossian, "that you came."

"OK. WHAT DO you want?"

Ossian stood four-square in front of Colin, who was hugging a marble fish to stop himself from toppling into the ornamental pond.

Colin's mind and voice were clear enough, but his body was not quite sober and his face was copper-green.

"You should have paid attention before, when I first warned you. It's much too late now."

"You're talking about Sue?"

Colin gave a round of slow, ironic applause. "Still taste her on your lips, can you? That soft tongue flicking?"

"Sod off. At least I'm not a pathetic loser spying through the grass. Is that how you get your kicks now, Colin?"

Colin smiled. "I wasn't spying. I was right behind you, over by the trees. Sue saw me well enough. Meant me to see, too. She wanted to show me just how deep she had her hooks into you." He lurched forward and made a grab at Ossian's arm: "I feel sorry for you though, my ghostly friend!"

Ossian took a moment to catch up. "You heard as well as saw then."

"I heard. Sue was spot on there, I'll grant her. You're virtually transparent."

Ossian said angrily: "You were the one who warned me off all that ghost stuff. You told me not to listen to her."

"And how I wish you hadn't! She's a siren, see? You shouldn't listen to sirens."

"You can't have it both ways! Do you really believe I'm a ghost? Are you as crazy as her?"

Ossian stepped forward with his fist bunched and bent Colin back over a tail with marble scales.

"All right," Colin winced. "I'll tell you. I'll tell you about the King's Head the other night. I thought I'd dreamt it at first, but now – now I don't think so. I was sitting outside the pub, looking up the lane. It was just getting dark when I saw *you*, Ossian, with the sunset red behind you and your shadow stretching out like a giant's. And I was about to call to you, only you were—"

"I was what?" prompted Ossian.

"Different. This will sound ridiculous. But your head was *glowing*. Like it was made of polished metal – all yellow and red. And then the sun ducked under the horizon You weren't there any more." He looked Ossian full in the face. "You vanished."

"Hah! I bet you needed another drink after that."

"Too right. But since then I've been watching you, Ossian. I've been on your case. You want to know what I think? Truly? I think you're the genius of the shore, my friend. I think you're part of the furniture here in Lychfont, the ghost of all ghosts."

This meant nothing to Ossian. He pushed Colin back further, till his head was dangling just above the water. But still Colin spoke.

"You've always been here. You *are* Lychfont."

Ossian scoffed. "I've only been here twice in my life!"

"You reckon? I thought you might have more of a clue. Where did you stay in America?"

"Philadelphia. You know that."

"Yeah? And what's it like, Philadelphia?"

Ossian corralled a few maverick facts. "You've seen it on the telly, haven't you? The Liberty Bell? Betsy Ross? Cheesesteaks?"

Colin shook his head. "That's what I'd get out of a travel brochure. I want to know what you *did*. Did you have a life there? Friends? You sure you didn't dream it?"

It was ridiculous. But for a moment, that dreadful blankness threatened to swamp Ossian's mind. The radio static that flared whenever he thought of America hummed and buzzed. Think! Philadelphia!

"Lizzy!" Ossian clutched at the name. "I had – I have – a girlfriend there."

Colin smiled thinly. "You sound relieved – but I bet you haven't thought of her in days. How nice to remember her now, though, as things start getting weird the Lychfont way. Lizzy sounds like a good, steady girl, the kind you could settle down with. A student, did you say?"

"She is and I didn't," said Ossian. He was still wondering whether or not to punch Colin in the mouth.

"Studying something reassuring like Social Sciences, perhaps, or Applied Upholstery."

"Art History," Ossian muttered.

"Not so far off the mark. What were we talking about again? Oh, yes, Philadelphia. City of Brotherly Love. That place you remember so well."

"If you don't believe me, ask my dad."

"Is he substantial enough for that? No, of course, Jack Purdey is a towering figure in today's landscape scene. Get real, Ossian – if you can! How large do you think you loom in his world? When he's here, your dad thinks he has a son called Ossian. When he's outside Lychfont, who knows? He's doing his watery thing. Pastels and gouache! You said it yourself – you're only here to make the scenery look good. Excuse me."

Colin paused to be sick into the pond. The vomit spread in cumbersome circles, then caught in reeds. Something bright-eyed and small was fritting beneath the surface.

"Don't you get it, Ossian? This place is heavy! It presses down! It takes strong minds and twists them like spaghetti round a fork!"

"Piss off, Colin."

"Don't believe me. No, no, you shouldn't. I'm not very trustworthy and this story looks about as likely as your dad winning the Turner Prize. So off you go; pretend to be a real person with a real life. I won't stop you. But just try leaving Lychfont and see. Head up the road into the forest. Put the Solent at your back and see if you can feel that hot wind shrinking skin to bone. See if the road bogs up to your thigh."

"Thanks for the tip, Colin. I'll try that some time."

"Don't leave it too long, Ossian!"

But Ossian did not go into the forest yet. He turned on his heel and walked along the path to the front of the house. The two-seater was parked near the porch, with a bare patch in the gravel where Jack had skidded to a halt a few days before. The metallic paint was growing dusty. And there was Jack himself, lumbering out of the house with a canvas under his arm and a holdall on his shoulder. He pointed the remote. The horn sounded twice. Lights flashed.

 OSSIAN WAS STANDING on the spongy lip of a bog. Moss grew under his feet and sedge, yellow and withered, speared the margins of the water. He dared not look behind him, for he knew that at his back a crowd had gathered – a crowd that was nervous and expectant. The people in it had come to watch him die.

Peering down through the midge-haze into the shallows, he saw the shapes of half-rotted branches and roots, tangled like corpses in the fine mud. The mud itself was streaked with dark lines and misty in the water, as if an object barely buried there had just stirred. *Was* stirring! Ossian gasped – the ripples of the mud pool thickened and the light coarsened as it fell on a rough, leathery arm. He saw the creature's elbow first, but it might have been a wrist, so impossibly long were its fingers, and so deceivingly folded with billows of dank, black skin. Those long fingers were forced to curl and bend at the edge of the bog; they reached up the bank and presented him with a row of tapered nails, and just below the water's surface a pair of round eyes blinked. Ossian backed in terror, but at the same moment he felt the soft edge of the bog slide from under him and he was toppling over, down and down.

"Shall I dip the napkin again?" said a female voice.

"No, no – let him wake. It's better he knows a little, as I say. Ignorance will never find the path."

"Well, keep that blade ready."

Ossian remembered now. A cloth had been clapped over his mouth. It had smelt foul but the foulness had made him sleep – so deep that it was not until the blade was tried against his neck that he blustered free of it.

He was not aware of having opened his eyes, but there, at once, were Susannah and Adam Price before him. Susannah was sitting upright in a high-backed chair. She was pale as chalk, but her eyes flashed. A flask stood on the table beside her, its neck bunged with yellow-stained cloth. And her wounds – the wounds he had felt bleed freely at his touch only minutes before – were dull, burgundy scars.

"How long have I slept?" Ossian asked.

"Long enough," said Adam, "and less than you shall. When you wake next it will be to St Michael's trumpet."

"And I'm sorry, brother, that it should be so," said Susannah.

"Susannah," croaked Ossian, "what have you done?"

"Adam *made* me tell," she said. There was weeping in her voice, though her eyes were dry.

"Tell *what*?"

"The secret of the elixir, of course! He wanted it so badly and I was afraid. So I told him. To come by the elixir there is only one way. A head – a head of bronze. A nameless boy." She was finding it hard to speak. "He wants the head from your shoulders, Ossian. He wants to slap clay across your eyes, to hear your bronze lips speak. And you will speak such things! Your head will prophesy so that the angels themselves will strain to hear."

Ossian looked from one to the other. Saturnine, heavy-set Adam Price was nodding gravely. Susannah smiled encouragement, as if she had brought him to the brink of heaven's bliss.

"You're mad! Both of you!"

Adam Price smiled dangerously. "Was Doctor Bacon mad?"

"Yes! Yes, he was mad like you!"

"You speak from ignorance. His spells would have raised a wall of brass round this island. His magic was strong and sound."

"There is no wall round Britain. That spell was a dream!"

Adam rose, his dark cloak hanging from his shoulders to his feet.

"It would have happened, sure enough. But Doctor Bacon's apprentice neglected his duty and let the Head he made shatter. I have been more watchful of you, Ossian. And what I seek is such a little thing, so little, but a morsel of curiosity." He opened his hands wide. "I would but know the truth of the world to come."

"And who but a dead man can tell him that, Ossian?" asked Susannah.

Ossian's head was clear enough by now for him to realise that he was no longer free to move his arms or legs. Adam had tied him as he slept, and he lay on the table he had seen when he came in. Only it was no table, but a cold, limestone slab.

"How easy it was to bring you here," said Susannah, "where the land is red. It must be bloodier yet, Ossian."

Her voice was muffled, as if he heard it from within the brass walls of a brazen skull. She's not even the same person, he thought. She's nothing like Susannah.

That was true. She was tall; her head touched the roof-tree of the house. And there was no house, just the roof of spread branches and the green, thick light he amazed himself by breathing. Then not even the forest was there: nothing but the stone block he lay on and, far away, Peg of the Willow lamenting her dead lad.

"It breaks my heart to mar his lovely flesh," said Susannah. Though he could barely see her now he saw enough to know that even her scars were gone from her and that she was divine – a Shining One. Adam too was changed. His manners were deferential and humbly obstinate, all his wiles become a kind of devious service to this goddess.

"Your tenderness is truly exquisite. But an Oracular Head can be come by in no other way. Remember, lady, this is not the *real* Ossian. Just a reflection, glinting on the dark ocean of—"

"—human history. Yes, scryer, I remember that speech. But I cannot love as mortals do, to change with every turn of the season. I must love Ossian eternally; it is my destiny and his death will always bring me pain. Therefore, despatch him and be done. I will look away."

She drew her cloak about her.

"Lady, you are a goddess that speaks it."

SUE HAD JUST come out of the shower. She sat on her bed in a white dressing gown, blow-drying her hair.

"You knew, didn't you!"

Sue turned and smiled vaguely, as if she had not quite heard him over the dryer. "Hmm?"

"Don't pretend! I can see through all of you."

"Oh," she said comfortably. "Hello, Ossian. Why don't you come and sit on the bed and we'll talk it over." She patted the cover next to her. The turquoise on her ring shone like a third eye.

"I'm not some lapdog you can just call to heel!"

"What's brought this on? There's no need to be unpleasant."

"I haven't even started yet! You knew! You knew Colin was watching, didn't you?"

"Colin?" Sue did a very passable impression of not understanding what he was talking about.

"When you kissed me. That was for his benefit, wasn't it?"

"You're being ridiculous," she said, as if to a petulant child. "Is this hurt pride talking? Why should I want to do that?"

"I don't know! I don't know what game you two are playing – but I'm not going to be part of it, all right?"

She stood and put the hairdryer back on her dressing table, then turned to him coldly. "It's a bit late for that, don't you think? Your father made a fool of himself last night. Now I'm beginning to think it runs in the family."

"What Jack gets up to is nothing to do with me. Nothing is. I'm not involved."

"Don't be stupid, Ossian. You've always been involved. And you've got business here in Lychfont you'll never be able to finish."

"That's where you're wrong. I talked to Dad just now. He's packing the car. He's had a call, a big commission up north. So we're off. You'll have to find someone else to play your mind games. Sorry to have slipped through your net."

"A big commission?" laughed Sue. "Is *that* what he told you? Jack's got a nerve, I'll grant him."

"What are you saying?"

"A big brush-off, more like. You should know him better by now, Ossian. There's no fool like an old fool – except, perhaps, a young one."

"You don't know everything!"

Sue gave a chilly laugh and grinned, showing all her frost-white teeth.

Ossian could hear her singing as he stormed out through the entrance hall, past the Stubbs bay and the tiger skin. Mr Frazer, busily transforming the driveway bushes into topiary goblets, looked up and followed him steadily with his gaze as he started across the lawn and down into the wood, making for the King's Head. Ossian had decided to phone for a taxi; Southampton wasn't far. And the path was unsteady with anger as he turned and set his face to the trees, away from Lychfont House. Away from all of them: Sue, Colin, Catherine, his father. He was going back to America and to Lizzy. He'd got cash in the bank, hadn't he? Enough for the flight. Lizzy had been right all along. He never should have left.

But he was no longer alone. Someone was tracking him through the wood. Didn't Colin know when to give up? And what was he carrying? A croquet mallet? A length of lead piping? Ossian laughed out loud. What would Inspector Gordius have made of it – or feisty Sergeant Rosie O'Shea? He laughed until his cheeks were wet. When he blinked the trees were empty. He felt light-headed. There was no sound beyond the green hissing of the leaves.

"You shouldn't have listened to her, Ossian! You shouldn't have looked!"

That was Colin calling! It sounded like Colin. But the voice was in his own head.

"If you touch the goods, you have to pay, you know!"

"Sod you!" cried Ossian and plunged into the wood. He ran. He felt the wind pull his skin back over his skull. The trees flicked, and in the shadows between ran black shapes, large as mastiffs, sinuous as otters. They were running alongside him, steering him, heading him off. Just shadows – shadows on the woodland floor. So he skewed his head to look, and one of the shadows turned its head too, and its mouth was dripping crimson, and the teeth were saw teeth, and the points of them were tipped with crystal. Ossian gave a shout and ran on into the heart of the wood. He flung himself along the soft earth track, choking on his own breath until the ground welled with bubbling mud and sank him, and the grass looped to make him stumble and he fell, and drowned in the sudden drenching pool...

...BUT WAS ALIVE. He had forgotten that the cord about his neck was twisted with a stick. It had crushed his windpipe, quite. His face had bloated and his eyes were shut. His wrists, loosely tied, floated above his head and occasionally hit the surface of green water, pocked with bubbles and the fall of leaves. That water was peaty and bitter, but when the sun shone it glowed with life, with lurking toads and snails, reeds bent and gluey with larvae. Fish ruddered by, and occasionally a crocodilian shadow would flow over Ossian's face – the wriggle of a newt.

A long time he lay, but not so long till the mud crept over his skin and gathered in the corners of his dreaming eyes and the waxy cap he wore was crowned with it. Ossian did not hear the drying of the bank as the river switched its course, how the reeds shrivelled and gave way to soil and children, how his head was circled with May dances. To him the reed was as the oak. The gruel of sorrel, mistletoe and thorn in his belly took root and thrust out a may tree miraculously, hung with snowy blossom in the spring, with blood-red fruits. It grew and died, and only the trunk was left unfelled, for the sake of the ghost who haunted it.

THE PESTLE was grinding. It had done so, steadily, for more than two hours... *scrape, scrape, twist scrape...* Between stone and stone it had crushed the vinegar sorrel, the shrivelled haws. And mistletoe, that lovely plant, whose oak-berries must be lopped with gold. Ossian had seen his father cut it at midwinter; the fallen sprig had been caught in fine woven cloth, being too sacred to touch the earth. Dried, ground down, those pearl-white berries would season his last meal.

This house had three doors. One door for each clan, one for each tributary stream. By turning his head, Ossian could see, distantly, the grove of willow and birch where Sulis raced her waters. But to turn that way hurt his neck. The cord that tied him chafed his throat badly and the head of Cernunnos sat heavy on his shoulders. So he looked straight ahead. There were children playing in the yard. Beli's sister ran fastest; he saw her fall flat, winded – and Beli sat on her and chomped the flesh of her arm. Then their mother shouted and told them not to hurt their luck by mocking at a god. The trotting dogs followed them away.

In the light-shafted, brown-aired house, Cernunnos sat upon the rushes with his legs crossed. A fire smoked in the central hearth and the smoke made a rough pillar, twisting up into the roof, where it was teased out on heaven's spindle. When he looked at it he could see shapes – shavings of dream, sent by the goddess to lead him forward. The staff in his hands rippled with wedged-shaped notches. At its base they ran as serpent scales. The scales grew rougher towards the head, until they curled and rolled, were more wool than scales, were wool. The snake's head was horned like a ram's. Such was his staff, to guide him over the grassy plain of dreams.

Inside the Cernunnos head Ossian was afraid. He had not been, to begin with. The gruel of sorrel and mistletoe had filled him with power at first. He had woken with the cup to his lips. Bitter, bitter taste, sharp as a sword, powerful.

"Look in the pool."

A man had stood beside him. They had been standing in a grove, with a pool at its centre. There were trees all around them and a green palisade beyond, the rushes cross-woven. But most of the trees were dead. They were gnarled and carved with mouths, horrible in their great age and stained with dark. They gaped for him.

He looked into the pool. Saw branches of tined bone, first, catch on the treetops. He did not realise they belonged to him, nor that they were antlers, until his head shook with the bitterness twisting in his mouth and he saw the branch bones shake too, and heard his name again.

"O Horned God."

And the face was his, and he was Cernunnos. Then the man who had spoken was known to him, as everything was known. This whitebeard had been his father.

"You have a journey," said the priest. "Your bride waits for you."

So. That dream-cinder paled to ash. Now others kindled. Fingers touched the great antlers, the fur on his face. Was that just a mask? Where was Ossian? Was he hiding within the god?

These questions did not catch; they flew from him like blown seeds.

He dreamt of the wagon. He had travelled through the apple land, the green lanes and the meadow grass, with his bride beside him. Her face was beautiful – her face and hands were crisp flowers, lavender, bee-visited: her eyes blue musk thistle and all her bones were fragile plaited straw. In those few days, spring met with harvest, green shoots and yellow wheat, and the mowers' chorus was everywhere. The memories came tumbling forward now. Garlands in the maybush! The woods had been plundered in their honour, and all were tied with marriage links for the wedding of Cernunnos and the Queen of the May. At each village gate they found a loaf unbroken, and the meal was sweet with honey, and— What was this? A child's fingers, straining to touch the fold of his robe? That picture had stuck – even down to the red nail-dirt, the milk-white quick. The child's face he never saw; she had been snatched from him roughly, as from a snake

In the house with three doors Cernunnos shifted from ham to ham. Now, had that been more like waking or sleeping? Waking, surely; he had never been more alive to every taste and sound. But to be tied to a post with a wicker mask upon his shoulders – to be awaiting the sword that would kill him – that must be some great, grey maggot of a dream. Not once, but three times he would be slaughtered. First with a golden blade, as befits a god. Then with a hemp rope – a thief's death for snatching at forbidden sights. At last, they would dedicate him to the ground, with a stave's blow to the skull.

After a week and a day the wagon had come full circle. It had brought him here to the village and the goddess had withdrawn to her island. The wagon itself, led by the slaves who had tended her, was drowned in the bog. A year had gone to its making; each spoke had been gilded and the bronze faces of the gods had peeped open-mouthed from between his knees as they had travelled. Now all was broken up and buried beneath hurdles in the brown water. Neither wagon nor slaves would be seen again.

Last night they had served him the sacred gruel a second time. But it had been too strong and he had retched up its magic. Now they held the boy Ossian, no god, though they did not know it. He would suffer, not fiercely and joyfully as a god should suffer, but as a mortal, in pain and desolation. He shivered. The slaves had not died quietly.

The priest came and began his catechism. Ossian had heard the same exchanges before. Now he must be perfect or his father would find that the god had deserted him.

"What is your name?" said the priest.

"I am Cernunnos."

"That is a lie, for Cernunnos is dead."

"He is alive and I am he that speaks it."

The priest nodded; that was right.

"The grey tent of the sky, will it fall?"

"See, I have propped my staff between earth and heaven."

"The brown leaf, will it shoot again?"

"I have ploughed the dead land and made it fruitful. I am the sower and the harvest."

"How long will the mayfly live?"

"A day and a night, which is the whole of time."

Through the eyeholes of the mask, Ossian could see his father's face. His father was not looking at him, but at the ground before his feet.

"The King and Queen, the Red and White – what shall their child be named?"

Ossian hesitated.

"I know that but I will not tell you," he replied.

Satisfied, the priest left at length. Ossian sighed with relief. He had remembered his answers well, even down to the ritual hesitation.

They came in the evening. Without the wagon he was forced to walk, but his train was kingly as he travelled the quarter-mile from the village to the Stone of Cernunnos. The priest was behind him, then the princelet of this valley and his guard. The village straggled at a distance. They left the roundhouse and made for the hill track, where it swung close to the river. He tried to walk like a god, with a god's ungainly stride, as if he were hobbled by this earthly form, a seed near to splitting. No one spoke, but there was a hand on his shoulder once or twice, to steer or steady him.

Here they were nearest the trees. And now he stirred himself at last and tried to save his life. He turned and snatched the priest's dagger from his belt. The old man crumpled and a cry went up – they thought he had slit his belly! But it was all right; the priest was just winded from the blow of the pommel. He was staggering forward, pushing offered arms aside, trying to form a name with rounded lips. But he fell. Even at that moment he fell and split his head on a rock. Twenty years of sacred learning leaked out on the stones. The man's mouth opened and welled with spit. The moss was ruddled with it.

A scream to left and right – but Ossian had fled to the wood, with the spears flying past his shoulder. No one dared follow. He made the cover of the trees, looked back and saw the hunters watch which way he would take. His chest pounded. They were watching, not chasing, but that made no difference. Soon they would come and find him in that grove. The god himself would point the way.

In the heart of the forest he put his palms under the wicker frame of the Cernunnos mask and pushed. The mask did not move. It seemed to have grown tight against his skin. He gripped and pushed again, up and round, wrenching it. Something cracked inside and four spear-sharp wicker sticks were stabbing his chin, jaw and neck. As he eased the frame upwards they sliced him till the blood ran. The mask was made cunningly. To remove it that way would be to pierce his windpipe, gaff his spine. He stopped, defeated. There was no other way: the deer skin was supple and slick to the touch, and sewn tight with shrunk twine he broke his nails in trying to unpick. The antlers rammed his head with bone, bucked as his head shook. He feared their magic; they belonged to the god himself, who was the King of the Wood.

He cried there for his trespass. Already the world was growing misty with the shades of dead men. He knew they awaited him. The sharp leaves hung down, moist with evening dew. They looked like blades, those leaves, copper-green and wood-hafted. He reached out timidly and touched one. Its edge was keen.

And there was Cernunnos himself, standing before him!

"Save me!" Ossian begged, and fell down before him.

He saw Cernunnos's great stag face, mocked in his own. His eyes did not blink. Was he angry?

"What is your name?" came the voice of Cernunnos. "Who are you afraid of?"

"My name is Ossian!"

The great stag face did not move, except that it rippled slightly with the breeze, for the face was only a reflection. Ossian had fallen at the edge of a reedy pool, black with sticky mud. It was himself he saw, himself grown mad through fear and poison and, as he stared, those torch-yellow eyes spread along the surface of the pool like fire through summer bracken and engulfed him.

A stick broke fifty paces to his left and waked him suddenly. Alert at once, he crouched deep where the rock cupped and he could not be stalked from behind. At the far side of the clearing the yellow grass shivered. Someone shook a rattle. Someone sighed.

"Ah, Cernunnos!"

One of the bushes had grown a long black snout. Among the yellow flowers two black-veined, cream-yellow eyes could be seen blinking, and nearby crouched a beast whose ears were flat against its skull. A threat, lighter than a bee's wing, burred in its throat.

By this Ossian knew that the hour of his death had come. Sulis had sent her hounds to fetch him, as was her right, being a goddess and implacable. The dogs stepped forward. He knew them all, for his father had taught him their names: Saw Tooth, Long Gut, Famine. They walked two-legged and they carried spears. Ossian saw the shadow of his antlers spill forward across the grass to touch their feet. Then he was kneeling and the Serpent Ram would no longer support him. It lay spurned at the far end of the clearing, where a boot had sent it. His fingers pressed down leaves.

Bright metal slithered from a sheath. Ossian did not wish to look up into that dog-mask, to know its eyes. He knew the eyes of all the village. He did not wish to know what friend had killed him.

But it was a stranger's voice that spoke above his head: "I was right, you see?"

Cheerful, pleased with itself, and intent on explaining how pleased it had a right to be. But it was not talking to him.

"Had we waited longer his spirit would have slipped away again. We were lucky to find him in time."

"He's a lovely-looking boy," sighed someone piteously.

"He is indeed, my lady. And he will make an exquisite corpse."

"This is the last? There'll be no more of these... expeditions?"

"I stake my reputation on it."

"More than your reputation, believe me. Now, don't chatter on, you magpie. Just slit that handsome throat and have done. I shall avert my gaze."

"As you will it, my lady, so shall it be."

THE FIRST THING Ossian knew about was his neck. That hurt
– not sharply but deeply, unforgivingly. His head had been
severed from his body, then stuck back ineptly with horse
glue, that was how it felt. The gash – from the seat belt? –
ran a long way, from his collarbone up to the far side of his
throat. He was curious in a sleepy way, but not enough to
care much.

He lay for a while, eyes shut, sampling the taste of the
pain, feeling his heart beat. His mind lay sour and shallow,
like a dish of summer milk. Then fearfully, half-
reluctantly, he edged his hand towards the hurting place.
But his hand would not move, not easily. It was swaddled
in something thick that took away all feeling. Bandages,
perhaps.

Just how badly hurt am I?

At last, it occurred to him to open his eyes. He had clean forgotten about them, silted as he was in pain and silence. He peeped through the mesh of lash and lid. Daylight: natural, not electric. Whiteness too – and cream in places, with a rectangular slice of blue that might be window-framed sky. He discovered that he had already known, from the echo of heeled feet upon the floor, that he was in quite a large and barely-furnished room, with high ceilings. Also, that he was not alone, though it took an age of bleary focusing to distinguish the woman in front of him from the wall and the sky, and the heavy, velveteen beauty of the roses that obscured her. Her face was turned from him to the light and all Ossian could make out clearly was the swirl of her hair where it foamed in bubbling curls about her shoulder. Not that he needed to see more; those curls identified her at once, even if the freckles were hidden.

"Lizzy? Is it really you?"

His voice sounded feeble and cracked. Instantly, she was beside him. She had crossed the room as swiftly as a breeze and her eyes were smiling. "Hello, errant boy. I hoped you might join us today."

Her kiss was cool satin on his forehead. How could he have forgotten? Wonderful Lizzy. His desire for her returned, fresh as it had been at first. It was more painful than any wound.

"What are you doing here, Lizzy? Where are we?"

"In Lychfont, of course," she smiled. "Don't upset yourself. I came to find you as soon I heard what had happened. The moment I could get a ticket, I flew. You gave us quite a fright."

"I did?" said Ossian, and his mind ran with unexpected comfort and relief. Lizzy had flown so far – at who knew what cost? – to see him! She was his lover after all... The force of his relief was unexpected, and in his weakened state quite overpowered him. His cheek was wet with sudden tears. Then he remembered the bandages and the pain in his throat. "How do I look? Am I a mess? Tell me the truth."

She regarded him steadily. The expression of those steady eyes seemed to shift more than once, as the watery light shifted, between love and something more distant, more poised and ironic. The face itself, however, did not change. What was she thinking? Perhaps Lizzy was right after all. He didn't understand her.

"You'll do," she said at last and pressed her lips upon his forehead as if pressing a seal into wax.

She had left the room probably. He was lying on his back, watching the light shy across the high white ceiling. It was reflected from some pool or ewer, and rippled by a breeze he could both see and hear, though in the room itself the air was still.

"I only remember..." he began. Then stopped. She was beside him again, all attention.

"Yes?"

"What's Colin told you?" Ossian asked cautiously.

"Colin? Why would Colin tell me anything?"

"But when I ran away from Lychfont, Colin was there." He looked at Lizzy's expression of bemused disbelief. "I don't blame him; it's not that."

Lizzy detached a hair from her sleeve. "No one's blaming anyone, as far as I'm aware."

"I think maybe he was following me through the wood. He's a bit crazy, I think. It's all to do with his sister..."

"Now you've lost me," said Lizzy. "What sister?"

"Sue Frazer, of course."

She looked at him in incomprehension. "Who?"

"Colin's sister. His older sister. She's— well, you couldn't miss her."

"Hmm. I think your mind is playing tricks. There is no Sue Frazer. You didn't run away. You never even got as far as Lychfont House. You had a car crash on the way from Heathrow. Quite a bad one," she added solicitously. "Don't you remember anything about it?"

"No! Or—" Ossian paused, letting the stirred mud settle. "Yes. Yes, I do. Something. Dad was driving here to

Lychfont, too fast. And I think we smashed through a fence on the road. At least..." He tried, feebly, to shake his head. It all seemed to have happened to someone else. "Is Dad all right?"

Lizzy gave a snort. "Your father? Walked away from it of course, with nothing more than a sprained thumb. His kind always does."

Ossian felt relief, mixed with a curious unease. Lizzy was keeping something from him, he was sure. Some hard truth, perhaps, he was in too fragile a state to be told.

"I had such strange dreams..." he said.

"About Colin and his sister, yes. The one you couldn't miss. Should I be jealous, Ossian?"

Lizzy did not look at him. She was rearranging the dusty flowers in their urn.

"She was a lot like you. I was thinking of you probably."

"Yeah, right!"

Ossian found that he wanted to tell her anyway. Not just about Sue, but all of it, while it was still in his memory. The torturer... the priest... He knew what she'd say, of course – that they were all images of his father. His unconscious mind was acting out his true desire to rebel against Jack's authority. Lizzy knew the Freud game.

She sat and listened, her freckles wrinkling in unmysterious distaste at the gory parts.

"Remarkable," she concluded. "What a murky stream the unconscious is, for sure."

"You're bored. Sorry – and now I'm whacked again."

Ossian did feel dreadfully tired.

"I'm not bored at all, honey. But I think you should stop talking now. You look so sleepy." She put her fingertips gently on his lids and closed them.

Ossian did sleep – dreamlessly. And when he woke again nothing had changed. There were the same flowers, perhaps a little dustier, the same pale veins of reflected light on the white ceiling, the bright blue sky beyond the window, and Lizzy.

"...so long to get you back," she was saying, and he had the impression she had been talking for some time. That was all right. He liked to hear her voice.

All the same, he began to ask himself: Why am I here in Lychfont House? How come I'm not in hospital? Perhaps I'm not as bad as I thought.

"I should never have left Philadelphia," he said at last. "I should have let Dad come back without me after all. I see that. You tried to tell me, didn't you?"

"Every way I could think of," she agreed. "We were made for each other, you know. I seem to have been telling you that for ever."

"I won't leave you again."

"I've no intention of letting you go," she smiled, and placed her cool hand on his. "You lovely fool."

He saw himself reflected in her eyes. Two miniature Ossians blinked and shone. His injuries were slight enough not to have disfigured him, he saw with relief. Indeed, since his last sleep the pain of them had ceased to trouble him much. Dear Lizzy, who had come so far to find him. How he loved her!

He told her so.

They kissed with no pain, much tenderness. As Ossian slept again she hung over him, inscribing each inch of his sweet face in the tablet of her memory. She sighed as if for pity – then, glancing up, saw her own face reflected in the looking glass.

The glass stared back.

Her skin was pale and without blemish.

The glass watched her move to the window, where the sun was making its western entrance. It saw her smile and splay her white toes against the stored heat of the tiles. On the rafters above her head, a sleek raven stared down sidelong.

In the courtyard below, the scryer's horse was bulging with packs and bags. The clerk was scurrying round it, tightening girths and knotting ropes, to little apparent effect. The clerk was no horseman, she surmised. The raven agreed; it fluttered to her shoulder at that moment, with a raucous guffaw. She took a fist of seed from the pocket of her gown and felt his rough, horny beak scratch at her palm.

The prospect of Lychfont flowed from her. At the hill's brim a line of mowers raised their scythes in salute. A pretty piece of rusticity. Then came the necessary hedges, the meadows lagged with river weed and the glutting flood. Her statues, their nets and tridents crossed protectively, guarded the lawns. But it was from the spectral fountains with their ghostly rainbow veils that she derived her greatest pleasure. In them, shifting and elusive, dream-like in their beauty, she found the fittest emblem of herself. Sue... Lizzy... Susannah. They had all been parts beneath her dignity – just multicoloured, momentary splendours, twinkling in the light of history. Yet even they implied something of the true Sulis, who was infinite and inexhaustible.

Lychfont was – yes – very beautiful. Holy too, this place of running water, and she had known it so long. *Was* it, and so was Ossian. She would plant that healing spring very soon. It would be a wedding present for them both.

"Is it blessed then?" Sulis asked aloud. "Am I to have him?"

The great fireplace, lined with the immortals' busts, looked benign: no more of those frightening, bared, dark teeth.

"That's all right then," she concluded.

She spoke with satisfaction rather than gratitude. Happiness was no more than her due, after all. She clapped for Alaris, and Alaris, milking ewes several fields away, heard the call and came running.

What a day! The whole adventure, now that it was so happily concluded, had begun to seem rather amusing. How like Ossian it was to fly into a last-minute panic! And then let himself be brought back in sulky disgrace, and kissed and wooed into good humour. She really could not be cross with him for long. It had been an escapade, that was all, a stag-night adventure. The lovely boy – and soon to be united with her for ever. She licked her lips hungrily. She could hardly wait.

The sun hung low now, a drop of blood-red fire running through the green veins of the forest. The grounds, she decided, must be dressed in all their finery. The horses must be groomed and their tails plaited, their manes and fetlocks tied gaily with ribbons, wreaths of blossoms woven for their necks.

"W-what is it, mistress?"

Alaris was panting in the doorway. Her skin was moist and pink and her dress, charmingly, was still hitched from her flight across the reedy fields.

"Make my chamber ready, Alaris. You know what to do."

"The green robe, mistress, or the pearl white? Turquoise sets your eyes off beautifully too."

"Then lay out the pearl white and don't vex me with questions. I have other matters to concern me."

Seeing Ossian in the bed nearby, Alaris said shyly: "Yes, mistress. And may I wish you joy?"

"Indeed you may, Alaris," Sulis replied complacently. "I thank you for it."

She gave Alaris her instructions and went to bed. After everything that had happened, she was fatigued and it was pleasant to think of all those preparations going on as she slept. Ossian had looked so peaceful too, bless him. And content; he knew he had come home at last. She bent to kiss those truant lips once more – then drew back on impulse, lest he wake. Let him slumber now, let him rest. Tomorrow will be time enough for kissing. Tomorrow there will be amorous games enough, and bridal bells, and marriage garlands too. The hour will not be long. Ah, yes, Ossian, wait until tomorrow. For that, my love, will always be our wedding day.

# The Fetch of Mardy Watt

## CHARLES BUTLER

*Mardy glanced round her room. Everything was as it should be. Everything... except for that sentence in her diary: Rachel Fludd is a witch! She could not remember writing it there.*

A fetch is haunting Mardy Watt. This spooky double has been in her room, it's fooling her friends and it's upsetting her life. Exactly who has summoned the Fetch and why it is picking on her, Mardy doesn't know - but she has to find out, before it takes over and replaces her completely.

*"A wonderfully creepy story. You will never see the world in quite the same way again."* Diana Wynne Jones

*"This is a marvellous, spooky, funny book, a fantasy like no other. Read it!"* Susan Cooper

HarperCollins *Children's Books*

# Calypso, Dreaming

## CHARLES BUTLER

*Calypso tucked her knees together and hooked her
hands round her shins. Other people, she had
begun to learn, had dreams that stayed dreams.
They were lucky, those people. Her dreams always
came true.*

The isle of Sweetholm seems like the perfect
retreat. A haven for wildlife, its near-isolation means
it is just too far away from the mainland to attract
the hordes of daytrippers that swarm to the beach
at the first sign of summer. Tansy, in particular, is
looking forward to spending the holidays there. It's
a chance to escape the mess back home, where
her experiments in magic went so horribly wrong.

But troubles cannot be so easily outrun, for
beneath Sweetholm's idyllic exterior seethes a
darker heart...

*"beautifully conveyed... [for] those who appreciate
something out of the ordinary."*
Times Educational Supplement

HarperCollins *Children's Books*